FIRECRACKER

ANGERA ALLEN

or locales is completely coincidental.

Editor Ellie McLove at My Brother's Editor

Formatted by Jessica Hildreth

Cover Design by Clarise Tan at CT Cover Creations

Cover Photo Shutterstock Licensed Photo

Proofreaders:

Petra with Love N. Books

Jennifer Guibor

Kim Holtz

Tanya Farrell

Marlena Salinas

Firecracker / Angera Allen. -- 1st ed.

978-0-9986829-4-5 Ebook

978-0-9986829-5-2 Paperback

DEDICATION

This book is dedicated to my daughter!
My daughter's the light of my life. There is nothing that
doesn't start or end with her. She's the reason I follow my
dreams and live my life to the fullest. She is my everything.

My Little Sunshine,
Thank you for being the best daughter and best friend I could
have ever asked for. Mama is so proud of you and the
amazing girl you are. Dream big little girl you are a rising
star!
Love Always,
Your Loving Mama

CHAPTER ONE

"It's fine."

You piece of shit.

"Ruby?" I cringe, hearing my *soon-to-be*-ex-husband dragging out my name probably hoping I'll fall for his shit and submit to him like a good little obedient wifey.

I try not to sound like a bitch but fail when I reply, "It's fine, Brody." *Fucking asshole.*

"Don't give me attitude, Ruby. It was your decision to move out while I was-"

I cut him off before he can start spewing his lines of bullshit.

"For fuck's sake, Brody. I'm not giving you shit. You *do* need to see your daughter. I agree. As I said, *it's fine.*"

God, one day. One day I will tell him how I really feel. One of these days when I'm mentally stronger I'll unleash fury on him, but right now I need my anger inside to keep me going and not go back to him.

Hell no, not this time!

"Hello... Ruby? Are you even fucking listening to me?" Brody raises his voice sounding irritated.

"Yes. You will be home a week earlier than planned and you want Isabella to be with you for the time you're home before you leave again. I got it," I say snidely.

The voices in the background are my queue to get off the phone. Probably one of the groupies. I was so fucking stupid to believe he was different. Different than all the men my mother brought home or even married. I thought he truly loved me but what he wanted was an obedient wife who does what he says with no questions asked.

"Ruby, when I get back we're having a talk. This little tantrum you're having needs to end."

I laugh. "*I'm* having a tantrum? You sharing your *wife* with your groupie and band mate or should I say, *best friend,* is *not* a fucking tantrum. You cheating on your *wife* is *not* a tantrum."

"Ruby. Lower your voice. You're overreacting. We *will* discuss this when I get home and not over the phone. I miss you and want my wife back. You're not ending this marriage. I'll see you soon." *The fuck you will...*

He continues like nothing is wrong. "Kiss Bella for me and tell her that Daddy loves her."

I answer annoyed, "Sure," before hanging up.

I put my phone down on the counter, gripping the kitchen countertop with both hands breathing in deeply trying to calm down.

"It's okay. I'm fine. I'm okay. Every thing's going to be fine. I got this!" I say, giving myself a pep talk but failing horribly.

Fuck no, it's not fine and hell fucking no I'm not okay.

"For fuck's sake. Get it together," I say looking up at the ceiling.

I try to say positive shit to myself throughout the day. It

helps to keep me going, moving forward in life even though my life sucks donkey balls right now.

I'm a twenty-six-year-old, newly separated single mom. Well actually most of Bella's life Brody has been gone either on tour, in the studio recording an album or he has just been too exhausted to deal with us, so I pretty much have been a single mom since the beginning.

Life isn't all peaches and cream. It has its ups and downs, but most of the time it's just draining. I'm so inside my head, beating myself up with all the bullshit Brody has told me throughout the years and of course all my own self-doubts. I try not to think about it, but every day I have that little voice questioning myself... *Am I a good mom? Am I doing everything I can to make her life good? Did I do the right thing? Blah Blah Blah...*

"Mama!" my three-year-old daughter's voice bellows through the house, coming from her bedroom. When I don't answer fast enough, she screams again but louder. "Mommy!"

I pinch the bridge of my nose trying to keep my shit together but fail when another scream echoes throughout my auntie's condo.

"Isabella Malone! Stop yelling. What?" I yell back from the kitchen.

"Where are you?" she answers in a whiny voice.

For the love of God, help me stay calm.

Taking a deep breath, I reply back in a calm but loud voice, "I'm in the kitchen where you left me just a couple minutes ago. If you want to talk to me, come here and stop yelling, *please*."

We've been living with my aunt Giselle, for the last few months. I grew up here, and it was the only place I knew I could come to and feel safe. I've been over this marriage for a couple years now but never had an out. Brody isn't going to let me leave him so easily and he sure as shit isn't going to be happy when he's served divorce papers.

"Mama, what's wrong?" I look up to see my beautiful baby girl looking at me with concern while holding her Princess Aurora doll.

"Mommy was on the phone with work stuff. Nothing to worry your little head about." I put on a fake smile.

"K, Mama."

"What did you need?" I ask.

"Mama, can you come help me?" she asks, moving her doll from one arm to the other.

When I see she's still not smiling, I bend down in front of her and ask, "What's wrong, bug?"

I reach both hands out to her tiny little waist while looking into her sky blue eyes and I smile. One thing Brody did give me is this beautiful baby girl. My Isabella, who was named after my best friend and her Godmother.

When she extends one hand up to my cheek, she smiles back. "Come play with me." Moments like this makes everything worth it. Her touch. Her smile. Priceless.

"Bella baby, I can't right this minute, but once I get dinner started, I'll come play with you, I promise."

"Promise?" she whines.

Smiling back at her, I reply, "Yes, my little bug, I promise."

I lean in to kiss her forehead before giving her a big hug and squeeze that makes her giggle.

"Ok, Mama."

Once I know Bella is out of ear's reach, I dial the only person I can count on no matter what.

When I hear my best friend scream, "Ruby Rube!" I let out a deep breath and smile. God, I love this woman. No matter how much time has passed between us, we're always linked like soul sisters.

"Ruby? Are you okay?" Concern is etched in her voice.

I try not to cry, but my voice comes out shaky. "Iz, I need you."

I hear shuffling of the phone. "Fuck! Are you okay? Oh, my God, is Bella okay? Where are you? What happened?"

I let out a sniffle and take a deep breath. "I... umm. I-"

Izzy cuts me off sounding upset. "Rube, you're freaking me out. Let me cancel-"

"NO!" I shout out.

I'm not one to ask for help. Shit, she doesn't even know I moved out or that I'm serving Brody with divorce papers. Izzy is a big-time DJ in New York, and lately, she has been dealing with so much of her own life drama that I didn't want to bother her. She is over dramatic and would have flown home, but I needed to do this on my own. Until now.

Izzy yells at someone, "It's my best friend, Ruby from back home. Give me a minute."

I stand up straight, push my shoulders back and with confidence say, "I left Brody, and I'm asking for a divorce. He's coming home in a couple weeks and will be served divorce papers. He only has a week or two before heading out again to meet the band in Texas. He will want to see Bella, but I need to be gone. I need to..." My voice cracks in anguish.

"I'll book your flight tonight. Just tell me when and you can come here. I got you, girl. Holy shit! You finally did it! I am so proud of you," Izzy says calmly.

Her words hit me like a punch to the stomach, unleashing the dam of tears. I should have told her sooner. It might have made things easier.

"I'm so sorry I didn't call or tell you. I just didn't want to bother you. You were on your Europe tour and then all the stuff that has been happing to you. I just thought I would be bothering you," I ramble.

Izzy's voice raises, "Rube, soul sisters for life, remember. No matter where I am in life, I will always be here for you. I love you and fuck yes, I'm mad at you, but I'm even more proud of you. I knew you would come around. We can talk about the details when we see each other but just know I'm here for you."

It's been close to five years that I've been pushing her away, or I should say Brody has alienated me from my friends and family. Keeping me to himself while breaking me down.

"I'm sorry. I'm sorry for so much," I squeak out through tears.

"Mama! You're crying."

I whirl around to see my girl standing there looking stressed.

"No, baby, Auntie Izzy has me laughing so hard, that I'm crying," I say with a fake laugh.

Just mentioning Izzy's name her face lights up with joy. "An-tee Iz! I want to talk to An-tee!"

"Okay, Bug. Hold on let me put you on speaker but it has to be quick, Auntie is working, and Mama needs to finish talking to her, okay?"

She starts jumping up and down. "Ok, Mama. Yay, An-tee!"

Izzy's laughing. "Bella bug! How is my little snuggle bug?"

I let them chat while getting myself together, putting that fake wall back up.

It's fine...I'm okay...

After Bella runs back down the hall yelling for her babies,

I put the phone back to my ear. "Sorry about that, I know you're probably working."

With the upbeat auntie voice gone she says seriously, "Rube, stop. Don't close back up. Text me the dates, and I'll handle everything. If you don't text me the dates within the next twelve hours, I will be knocking on your aunt's door. Seriously, you need to get away, and I'll handle everything."

I swallow the lump that has formed in my throat. I want to cry again. She has always understood me. I reply, "Thank you. I love you. I really need you."

"Did he hurt you? I need to know if he physically hurt you. Is that why you finally left him?" Izzy's voice is so low that it catches me off guard.

"No, nothing like that. It's a lot of things and a very long story that will need a lot of alcohol and no baby girl to interrupt us." I end with a laugh thinking of my little spitfire down the hall, who's still yelling at her babies.

"Okay, I'm a call away. I can't wait to see you! It will be like old times."

I giggle just thinking of all the crazy shit we've been through.

"I hope so. I miss you too and thank you," I reply.

After we hang up, I finish dinner. And like I promised to, I play babies with my little bug.

CHAPTER TWO

Over the last couple of weeks, I filled my time with lots of preparing, moving schedules around and overall planning. Izzy has called every day checking to make sure I wasn't going to back out, and with my aunt's help, we made it happen. I leave today, and I'm so nervous, feeling on edge about everything that I feel sick to my stomach. I pray Brody doesn't flip out or lose it in front of Isabella while I'm gone. I know my daughter is in good hands with my aunt and his folks, but it scares me what Brody will do once he sees the papers.

Brody is scheduled to fly home tomorrow, but I don't know what time. My plan is to be in New York before he even lands in Los Angeles. As always, he never tells me when he is actually flying in. Before it was always to surprise me, but as of late, I think it is to catch me off guard. I'm clear headed and determined to end this with him. I just need him to understand that it is truly over. Once he does, we can start the process of the divorce.

"Mama?" Bella says in a whisper.

I reply, "Yes, baby girl," while turning to face her sitting next to my suitcase. Once I see she is upset, I drop my toiletries and move toward her saying, "Bella bug, what's wrong?"

I know what's wrong, but I still have to ask. Trying to hold it together myself, I pick her up hugging her tight against my chest. I'm just as upset about leaving her as she is of me leaving but I need to stay strong. This isn't my first time leaving her for a long weekend. But under these circumstances, we are both freaking out, and it's breaking my heart, because it's different, and she knows it.

"Bug, I'll be back in a few days. You're going to have so much fun with Daddy while I'm gone that you won't even miss me. I promise. Mama just needs to see Auntie and have some adult time." Still holding her, I sit down on the bed and lean back to look at her face.

She isn't crying which is a good sign, but the sad look on her face guts me.

"Mama, Daddy is going to miss you too."

I smile. "I know, little bug, but Daddy needs his Bella time. He has been gone for a long time and wants to spend time with you." I grab her small hands that are clasped around my neck and bring them in front of my face to kiss them.

"Plus, I'll be home in a couple days, and we'll have time to see each other before Daddy takes off again."

I know my daughter is smart and somewhat gets what is going on but hopefully, Brody doesn't make things worse this weekend. I haven't talked ill of him or said anything bad about him to anyone.

"Bu-but I want to go see An-tee Iz too. Why can't I go?"

I touch her nose. "We've talked about this. Mama needs some adult time, and with Daddy home, I can go have some.

Daddy's home from work and he really wants his time with you."

And, just like that her face changes, lighting up with a smile. "I can't wait to see Daddy."

I hug her so she doesn't see the hurt and sadness in my face. "See you won't even miss me."

———

I leave Bella with my aunt and hitch a cab to the airport. I've made it through security and I'm now in a bathroom stall crying. Anxiety is a bitch, and she's choking the shit out of me. Crying like a fucking baby, I fight with myself, 'should I go or should I stay' constantly second guessing my decisions.

When I hear my phone, I scream, "Answer the phone!" I know it's Izzy calling.

I try to clear my throat before answering and before I can say anything I hear Izzy singing, "Ruby Rue, where are you?" using the theme song from Scooby Doo. It always makes me laugh.

My laugh sounds somewhat normal. Hoping to mask how I'm feeling.

"Girl, are you at the airport? How are you doing? You better not be crying in the fucking bathroom."

Damn, this girl knows me. *Soul sister's for life.*

I answer all her questions with a shaky giggle. "Yes. Not good. Yes."

Izzy gets quiet and says in a serious tone, "I got you, Rube. Just get here, and let me help you find yourself again. It's just a few days of music, fun, and no drama. Now, are you out of the stall yet and on your way to the gate?"

Laughing, I stand up from the toilet I've been sitting on and move toward the sink.

"Because if not I'll stay on this phone until you do."

"Yes, I'm at the mirror cleaning my face. See you in a few hours," I reply.

———

The plane ride was good but filled with more anxiety.

Jesus Christ, I need to get a grip.

I'm like a fucking walking time bomb ready to explode. I have so much anxiety right now that I can barely breathe. Shit, I never used to be like this. I was always the fun, carefree, 'let's do whatever,' kind of girl but not anymore. I've always depended on people, first Izzy and then Brody. Brody was always with me, never letting me out of his sight and then there was Isabella. I don't think I've ever been alone.

I started stressing about Gus, Izzy's security guard picking me up. Izzy is DJing tonight at some lounge and can't pick me up. I shouldn't be stressed, I've met Gus a couple times, but it was always with Izzy. All I can remember of him was he was really big, had an amazing Irish accent and was scary quiet. Brightside, I shouldn't have a hard time finding him. I still feel weird about it being just the two of us.

I'm so excited to see Izzy DJing in a big club this weekend. It's been years since I've seen her in her element. I haven't even been to New York yet to see where she lives. My life has been consumed with Brody and Isabella. I need my best friend.

It's snowing in New York, so I had to go buy a new warm jacket. Izzy said she would loan me some clothes, but I still went shopping. I struggle to pull on my new big fluffy jacket and drop my bag. I didn't want to check any luggage, so I crammed all my shit into a big purse-like bag and a small rolling carry-on.

I'm leaning down to pick up my bag when two big black steel toe boots come into my view. I look up and see a black journeyman jacket which makes me lean back. I crank my neck up even farther to see the man's face.

"Ruby ...?" His voice is a deep rumble.

I know it's Gus instantly. *Yep, that accent, so yummy.*

I smile sheepishly. "Yes. How'd you know?

He smiles. "The hair." He points to my mane of wild sandy blonde hair.

Ah. He means, 'stuck my hand in a socket' hair.

"Perfect. Hi, Gus," I finish.

He tilts his head up in reply before saying, "You ready? Me boys outside waiting."

His accent has me in a trance, so I just reply with a head nod back.

"Is that all ye got?" he asks, pointing to my rolling carryon.

Good God, he makes 'you' sound so cute.

Still staring at him, I throw my purse over my shoulder before saying, "Yep."

When he leans down to grab it I try to stop him. "I can carry-" But he gives me a look, and I shut up.

He starts for the exit, only pausing a second for me to catch up. He's wearing a big black hooded sweatshirt with a journeyman jacket over it, making his chest and arms look even more massive. Don't even get me started on his buns of steel. The man's a fucking giant next to me. I bet Izzy wouldn't mind being his Jack if she could crawl up his beanstalk. I know she has a thing for him and damn he's tall enough for her. I smile holding in my chuckle, but he just nods and turns to walk away. One of his strides is like ten of mine, so I speed up my pace.

Walking through the exit doors, the warmth of the airport slipping away while a big gust of wind almost knocks me over. Ice. Cold. Wind. Wind we don't get in SoCal.

"Holyfuckingshitballs, it's cold," I sputter through clenched teeth.

Gus makes a humph noise but still not a word. I'm assuming it's his way of laughing. Freezing, I pull my hood over my head, cinching it around my neck. My hair is flying everywhere, so I try to shove it into the hood but fail horribly.

He motions toward a monstrous truck pulling up to the curb. It's slightly lifted but completely blacked out so I can't see the driver or anything inside. A matted gunmetal paint job and custom grill makes it look clean as fuck. I pause, not sure how I'm going to jump into this big fucker.

Gus moves toward the truck. I look around the airport noticing people dodging for cars to escape the wintery cold weather, horns are honking, and all my senses are on high alert, making me jumpy. Thank God it's not snowing right now. I close my eyes turning my face up toward the sky and say a little prayer.

I move toward the truck and when I'm a few feet away, the front door swings open with a male voice, who sounds irritated, barking from inside.

"Redman, hurry the fuck up. It's colder than a penguin's balls."

Ah-huh, Redman. I can see that with all his red hair.

Gus says something to the person when he opens the cab door, throwing my carry-on into the back seat. I can't see the driver because the truck is so goddamn tall. Horns honking all around me again has me jumping.

Gus turns around and motions for me to get in, but I look at him and then the back seat.

"How am I supposed to get in this fucking beast?"

Gus doesn't say anything, but the driver yells from inside the cab. "Jesus Christ, Redman, pick the little marshmallow up for God's sake, or something. My boy is going into hiding it's so fucking cold."

Boy? Ah, we have a comedian.

When Gus speaks, his voice comes out calm, soothing and not barbaric like the asshole driver. "Ruby, let me help you get in. Unless you want to try to climb in but I don't recommend it."

Gus smiles at me trying to make me feel comfortable, but when he moves behind me placing his enormous hands on my hips, I freeze. When he lifts me up my jacket moves upward shifting my hood over my face. I squeal, grabbing my purse and trying to see where the seat is but can't with all my hair covering my eyes.

It's so damn dark inside the truck that I can barely see two inches in front of me. Plus my jacket is so big and fluffy I can't move around. *Where the fuck is the dome light in this fucking truck?*

Gus shuts the cab door and jumps into the front by the time I get my purse off my shoulder, and my hood flipped back.

The driver has on a hooded sweatshirt with a baseball cap on backward but I can't see his face since he's looking over his shoulder trying to merge back onto the road.

"Get the fuck out of my way, motherfucker. You're lucky I don't just run your little Honda ass over."

Gus turns around in his seat. "Ya alright? Don't fret about this wanker. He'll get us there alright."

I try to smile but just sit there. I move around feeling for the seat belt. I feel like I'm in a cave sitting behind the passenger seat. When the driver finally turns to face forward giving me a view of the side of his face I see he has a strong masculine jawline. Since he is wearing the cap backward, I can't really see his hair, only the shaggy curls that hang out from under the cap.

Gus says from the front seat. "Quick, this is Ruby. Ruby, my man here is Quick."

Quick. Weird name.

Quick glances back a few times, he probably can't see me anyways through the darkness it would be a miracle. But, holy shit! I can see him. He's beautiful. Good God, I love me some facial hair.

I blink a few times. He could pass as fucking Brad Pitt with those blue eyes and that facial structure. *Damn, look at those lips.* Looks just like him and I silently gasp.

It must not have been so silent because Quick looks back right after and says,"Hi."

I don't reply but just stay fixated on that bottom lip.

Quick smiles and I lose all speaking ability.

"Jesus Christ, is she even back there? You still have your hood over your face? All I see is blonde hair. You okay?"

Jesus Christ is right.

Gus wrenches his big body around to check on me. "Ruby, ya alright?"

I snap out of my lust induced haze. "I'm okay. Sorry. Hello, why the fuck is it so goddamn dark in here?"

Quick keeps smiling but turns back and looks straight ahead at traffic.

"I don't like people to see what's going on inside here. I like it dark."

My sarcasm springs to life and I snap back. "*You* must *not* like seeing what's going on in here *either*, it's so dark in here."

Both men laugh. Quick leans forward touching the screen on the dashboard. "I can see just fine." He turns the music up, and they both look at the road.

A few minutes later I feel my body start to sweat with all these layers on. The seat feels like it has a heater blasting under it and my body is on fire.

Squirming around, I unbuckle my seat belt and try to unzip this oversized jacket.

"Is there any way I can get you to turn down the heat? I'm hot as fuck back here."

Quick doesn't turn back but leans forward again to the controllers. "You're hot as fuck alright."

What did he just say?

Gus tilts his head to face Quick. "Don't even think about it."

Quick glances at Gus, "What? I can't look?"

He can look...look at what?

Gus growls, "Iz, will knock you the fuck out boy."

Quick shifts in his seat peering back at me. "I'm just agreeing with what she said, right Ruby?"

When I don't reply, he winks at me and turns back to face the road.

"So... Iz says you two are like sisters. Grown up together and shit, so why didn't we meet you when we were in LA touring?" Quick questions, changing the subject.

Well, I was traveling with my husband. Having a foursome and finding out he is a cheating bastard.

"I was traveling with my *soon to be* ex-husband." My reply comes out bitchy just thinking of that son of a bitch.

Quick looks back for a second. He either figured out with

the tone of my voice, or he could see my face that it wasn't a subject I wanted to discuss.

"Well, you didn't miss anything except drama with a capital D." He shakes his head looking at traffic.

I humph in reply. *Oh, I'm sure I had just as much drama.*

Gus saves the day by changing the subject. "We're headed to White Wolf Lounge, where Iz's playing right now until she gets off at eleven. I'll take ya to her when we get there."

I nod my head but realizing he can't see me I reply, "Yes, okay."

The rest of the ride goes smoothly. The men chat amongst themselves, and I just stare out the window hoping I made the right decision by coming here.

CHAPTER THREE

We pull up to the lounge, there are a few men standing around out front but other than that it looks like a regular bar. Gus jumps out, opening my door next and when I move to the edge of the seat, I get ready to jump, but he moves in front of me reaching both arms out like he's going to catch me.

"Gus, I can jump out," I explain.

"Fuck no ye can't. It's all ice here an the last thing I need is for ye to crack that crown on my watch."

Before I can protest, he reaches in, gripping my hips again and pulls me out, placing me on the ground effortlessly.

I hear a whistle from the other side of the truck. "What the fuck you two doing? It's cold. Let's go."

I grab my humongous purse throwing it over my shoulder and yank my hood over my head before I take a step. It *is* slippery as fuck. I move slowly toward the door where the group of men are standing. Thank God I wore my Uggs.

I feel Gus move up behind me placing his hand on my lower back. "Follow Quick an I'll be right behind ya. He'll lead ya to Iz."

When I moved up next to Quick, I hold my hood in place

while I look up. He must have been staring at me because when our eyes meet, he smiles, letting out a chuckle. Jesus, he took his hat off letting his light brown hair fall into his face when he looks down.

"Fuck me. You look like a marshmallow with that hideous jacket on. All I can see is this big as fuck jacket, big ass boots, blonde hair flying around and tiny little legs moving."

I laugh. "Well I'm not used to this weather and need all the warmth I can get."

Goddamn, he's cute. He is just shy of Brody's height, but man he's built. Stop. Do not compare the two.

Quick opens the door and moves in only to stop a few feet inside the door, which in turn has me running right into the back of him. I shift my hood off to look around.

"Quick, head to Iz," Gus barrels from behind me.

"You got it, brother," he replies.

Once Quick starts moving, I notice it is standing room only. The place is packed. I don't see anyone in front of me with Quick being so tall and broad. I hear Izzy squeal before I see her.

"Ruby, Rube!"

Excitement and joy fills my heart for the first time in months. Before I have time to look around, Quick is being pushed aside, and Izzy's five-foot-eleven glorious model of a body is grabbing me into a bear hug.

"Finally. You're here!" she exclaims.

Quick laughs. "What, no hug for me? No, 'thanks Quick for going to get my girl?' Nothing?"

Izzy releases me to arm's length, looking me up and down. "Rube, what the fuck are you wearing? I can barely see you."

Both men laugh, but of course, it's Quick's sarcastic ass

who keeps talking. "See, I said the same fucking thing. She looks like a fucking marshmallow."

I laugh and hug Izzy again. I haven't said anything, and I'm trying to hold my shit together. I don't want to cry in front of all these people. Izzy must sense it too from the way I have a death grip on her, so without a word, she just turns around, ignoring everyone and pulls me hand in hand with her.

The crowd moves, letting her pass through. I don't look around, I just keep my face down looking at her three-inch heels clatter across the floor.

She opens a small door to a hallway and then another, and when I look up, we're in a small room with music equipment. Izzy lets go of my hand closing the door behind us, shutting everyone out. I just hear the music that is playing. Not knowing what to do or say I just stand there gripping my purse.

"I got you. Get your shit together while I play the next song. You got this girl," Izzy says, passing by me, heading toward the decks.

She puts her headphones on, turning her back to me, and that's when I see the mass of people dancing in front of the window-like wall. I turn to the side so they can't see me and move toward the couch. I drop my purse onto it before dropping my ass into it, and take a few deep breaths.

I'm here. Finally. I am here. I got this. It's like old times. Don't think too much into it. It's Izzy.

I put a smile on my face, wipe my eyes and sit back. Izzy is as beautiful as ever. She was supposed to be a model like her mother but hated it. She's a good ten inches taller than me on a good day but with heels on, she towers over me. She has her hair in Princess Lea side buns. I laugh thinking of all the weird hairstyles I've seen her do. God, she looks the same, if not better.

I start to relax watching her bounce around and tap her foot to the beat. She truly is an amazing DJ. As far back as I can remember, she always has been.

I look around at what looks like it used to be an office, but they knocked out half of the wall that is joined with the main lounge. Kind of like a bar, giving the DJ privacy but is able to interact with the crowd. They can't get in here or touch her, but they can talk to her if she wants to chat.

Feeling better, I stand up and see that the small dance floor is packed with people, with more people standing around their tables moving to the music as well. When she pulls her headphones down around her neck, she looks to me with a smile and then out to the crowd she starts to giggle. I hear a beat I don't recognize, but with Izzy, you always have to wait for her to drop the chorus to figure out what the song is and sure enough, "How I Could Just Kill A Man" by Cypress Hill, drops in the song. I laugh out loud. The song has obviously been remixed but sounds great.

Izzy laughs over her shoulder. "I knew that would get you laughing."

I start to dance to the song, moving my upper body side to side to the beat, bobbing my head. I unzip my huge parka jacket that goes all the way down to my knees. I laugh because now that they've said it, I do look like a marshmallow. I'm still moving my body to the music while fixing myself as much as I can. My hair is crazy wild since I didn't do anything to it but wash it today. I try to tame it down, but without product, the waves will stay wild.

I never did have the good hair like Izzy. She has beautiful blonde hair that styles perfectly, and then you have my sandy blondish brown hair that has wild waves to it, so styling it is a mission. I usually try to straighten it or curl it but as of late haven't done anything to it. The last six or so months, I barely got out of bed let alone styled my crazy hair. Nope, it's been buns, and ponytails for this girl.

Izzy turns around and smiles. "There's my girl. Jesus that jacket was swallowing you up." She laughs and begins dancing over to me, where we begin to bounce around each other singing the lyrics like we did back in the day.

"You know I don't do well with cold. Um, hello, in SoCal it's never this cold. I had to get something." I laugh.

Izzy moves to hug me. "That you did girl- that you did. I'm so glad you're here. You doing okay? How was the ride here?"

I hug her back, feeling the warmth of her surround me before we both sit down on the couch. "It was good. That guy Quick is a mouthy little shit isn't he?"

Izzy throws her head back laughing. "That he is," she states. "Quick's one crazy fucker, but I love him." She pauses. "I have a couple more hours to play. Remember me talking to you about Ginger, the one I went on tour with? She's out there in VIP if you want to hang out and get some drinks, or you can stay in here. Either way is fine with me. I just want you to have a good time and relax."

I can see the worried look on her face, but I smile and reply, "I got this. I just needed to get my bearings. I need to fix my face and check in back home, but then it's time to drink."

Izzy's face lights up. "That's my Ruby Rube. I'll have Gin come in here so you two can officially meet. Her man, Shy, and cousin, Mac, own this place. The boys are on strict orders to watch over you tonight."

Izzy gets up moving over to the door, opening it she leans

out saying something to whoever is standing outside of it. I grab my purse and fish through it for my makeup.

"Do I look okay? I have on Uggs."

Izzy turns around. "You look super cute. That sweater hanging off the shoulder is sexy."

I start to apply makeup while Izzy moves around the small area. I try to hold in my nervousness, but when I see a drink come into my view, I laugh. I thank the gods above for this woman right here, as I grab the glass from her. No matter how much time has passed between us, she knows me better than I know myself, and alcohol is the one thing I need right now.

Izzy states, "I think you need a couple of these right now before you do anything."

I smile standing up. "Iz, you know me so well. God, I love you."

She raises her glass to mine. "To finding you and to making new memories. Cheers biatch."

"Cheers biatch," I reply.

I slam down the vodka Red Bull. *Goddamn, that's strong.*

————

After I made my phone call home, talking with Isabella and downing another vodka Red Bull, I was feeling pretty good. Izzy's friend Ginger came in and took charge of me. Dragging me around the bar introducing me to everyone she talked to. We hit it off right away. She's sarcastic, full of hell and doesn't take any shit from anyone.

God, I used to be just like her. I want to be like this again.

I'm sitting in the VIP area buzzed from all the drinks everyone keeps handing me. I'm sitting next to Ginger and her man. I learned he's the president of the motorcycle club, called the Wolfeman, *which* Gus and Quick also belong to. Ginger is very friendly and keeps me up-to-date with who is who that walks by us. Izzy has mentioned a few of these people but nothing in detail. Usually, when we talked on the phone, it was where she was, how music was going, Bella and just overall updates on our life. Short and sweet, that way I didn't have to deal with Brody bitching. Brody didn't like how I acted after chatting with Izzy, saying I would be bitchy or sad. Probably because deep down I wasn't happy and talking to Izzy just reminded me of all the things I was missing out on.

Gus has been hovering around me but not saying too much. He gives me head nods here and there, but that is all. Most of the guys stand around the VIP area bullshitting and watching the crowd. The last hour I've been people watching myself and love it. It is so different here compared to back home, that it draws me in.

The one person I haven't seen since we got here is Quick. I've been scanning the crowd, but with so many people here it is impossible to find anyone. Especially with how short I am, being a little over five foot has always been an issue. I can never see anything when we're in a crowded group. I look to the booth and see Izzy smiling back at me. She has been killing it on the decks tonight. She's changed so much since the last time I've seen her, and I can't even remember the last time I've seen her perform. We have always loved music. I feel that's what brought us together all those years ago. She was the rich kid who was running from her parents, while I was on the poor side pretending to be rich. She has always been so beautiful but never acted like it.

I wipe the tear that falls just thinking about all the good times we used to have and how much I've missed her.

When Shy, Ginger's man, gets up to move behind us to

chat with a group of guys, Ginger grabs the bottle of vodka and moves closer to me. She takes this opportunity to let all the gossip start to spill. She pours us both a drink and dives in telling me about all the craziness this past year has been. I knew it was bad, but I didn't know it was this bad. I didn't know someone was killed and taken. Shocked, I slam the rest of my drink.

Jesus and here I am feeling bad about my shit these past few months, and they lost a friend.

Ginger pours us another stiff drink and continues telling me about her father's club and how she left there at nineteen to move here. How Shy was her first love and then her first heartbreak.

"For fuck's sake," I breathed, slamming back half of my drink.

She's telling me about how Shy took over an MC club here in New York, so he could be with her. It all sounded crazy, but it kept my mind off my own problems. I reply with my support for her and shock over all that she is telling me.

Goddamn, this woman has been through so much. I slam the rest of the drink.

She pours us another drink. I love watching her tell me the stories but when she keeps going on about being chased by bikers, fights in the club and when she told me about a finger being left for her, I freaked out and told her to shut the fuck up.

I'm completely buzzed and obviously feeling comfortable with her because I start to let loose about my fucked-up marriage. I don't tell her much, just how stupid I feel for being so upset over the fuckwad when they have been through so much more. We go back and forth with stories, and before long we are both totally shit faced, laughing, talking shit. I can't believe all the shit that has happened. It's shocking, and I can't think straight.

I slam my drink and sit back in the chair, trying to wrap my head around all the shit she just told me when all of a sudden Ginger jumps up. I bolt up after her ready for anything, especially after what she just told me, but there is nothing.

"Ruby, let's dance," Ginger yells all amped up.

"Fuckin' hell, Gin, you scared the shit out of me. I thought there was a fight or someone coming to kill us."

I clench my chest and start to laugh at how silly we probably looked. Moving around so fast has all the alcohol rushing to my head, and I get light-headed.

"Easy Gin. Don't make the lass throw up," Gus says from next to me when he grabs my elbow steadying me.

All I can do is giggle and try to focus on standing up straight.

"Sit down. Let me get you some water. Gin, watch her an sweet Jesus, don't give her anymore to drink," Gus growls.

I fall back into the chair now hysterically laughing. Ginger moves in front of me dancing, she leans down placing her hands on either side of the big lounge chair.

"Oh, my God. Are you okay?" Ginger says giggling.

I keep laughing. "Hell yes, I'm okay."

I lean back in my chair with a smile, thinking how this woman just woke me the fuck up.

Fuck. I've been in my own head for so long that I didn't take the time to look around. There are other things going on in life that are way worse than what I'm going through. I'm just getting divorced. My life isn't over. Things *will* be okay. I *will* be fine. Shit, my life is just beginning.

Feeling good about myself and my little pep talk, I try to stand up to dance with Ginger but fail, falling back into the big cushion chair. Ginger comes to my aid, but we both just end up laughing trying to get me out of the chair to dance. Shy comes up behind Ginger grabbing her around the waist lifting her up. She squeals laughing, yelling at him to put her down.

I lean forward placing my hands on my knees, taking a deep breath. I see Gus moving toward us from the bar. I take another deep breath and try to pull myself up out of this fucking chair when suddenly I'm lifted up effortlessly by two strong hands that come from behind me.

Who the fuck?

"Jesus Christ, woman, you're tiny as fuck without that marshmallow engulfing you. And this fucking hair..." Quick says, purring next to my ear before taking in a deep breath.

Jesus, Quick! Did he just smell my hair? His breath on my neck sends a wakeup call to every nerve in my body.

I swing around losing my balance and falling back, but Quick reaches out catching me as he pulls me into

his massive chest. I place my hands on him, leaning back to look up at his face and spout off, "For fuck's sake quit calling me marshmallow."

Quick's smile widens showing me his pearly whites. "You're a feisty little shit," he drawls sexily.

I'm dizzy, and it isn't all from being drunk. *Fuck, he's fine.*

"You always this feisty or is it just me you like to fuck with?" Quick says down at me with a devilish smirk.

How can anyone talk to him when he looks so good I want to devour him. I know it's been a while but Jesus if he doesn't have my lady parts stirring to life. Quick starts to chuckle under his breath, and I realize I haven't answered him.

"I'm a bitch to everyone," I huff, giving myself a high five for making a complete sentence without slurring.

"Oh, darlin', you're anything *but* a bitch. This little fire you got spouting out of that sexy little mouth of yours has my body blazing. I was hoping it was just for me," Quick rasps out, lowering his hand to the middle of my back giving me a squeeze tighter against him, letting me feel his massive erection pressed against his jeans.

I feel my face heat up, but I can't take my eyes off his baby blues. Goddamn, those things could hypnotize a fucking nun, they're so mesmerizing to look at.

Izzy's voice towers over the crowd. "Quick, you bothering my girl?"

He smiles over my shoulder at what I'm assuming is Izzy charging toward us. He leans into me, lowering his face to my ear and whispers, "Have fun with your friend, I'll be seeing you later."

Quick slowly let's go of me but not before making sure I can stand on my own. I hear Ginger still yelling at Shy to put her down behind me.

Goddamn, that man's tempting. It was like in Thelma & Louise when Brad Pitt first said hello to Thelma at the car. Best movie ever... *"I want him. Please, can I have him?"* I giggle to myself.

I realize that I'm just standing there staring at him walking away from me when I see Izzy move up next to me also watching him walk away.

Izzy's smiling, so I know she isn't mad. "You can if you want."

"Shit, did I say that out loud?"

"You sure did. You good?" Izzy replies.

I smile in return. "Oh, yeah. I'm good."

Ginger yells, "I'm not. Put me down, Shy."

She giggles trying to hit him on the ass but failing horribly.

Shy laughs playfully. "You keep shaking that ass in the air, it's going to be spanked, you hear me?'

Ginger giggles, replying, "Promises. Promises."

Shy sets her down kissing her forehead. Ginger smiles up at him, then smacks him on the shoulder. As she starts to move toward us, we all hear a SMACK. Ginger's face turns bright red, but she doesn't make a sound. She just wiggles her ass and keeps walking toward us girls.

"What the fuck? I leave you two alone for a while, and you're both shit faced, getting into trouble."

Ginger huffs, "We were just sitting there, and I wanted to dance. He didn't need to get all caveman on my ass."

Izzy crosses her arms over her chest. "You had your ass in the air bouncing around while you were bent over talking to Ruby. *And,* when I saw Gus rushing to the bar for water, I knew one of you two were in trouble."

We both look at each other.

"What? I'm not that drunk." Ginger sounds somewhat normal. *Bitch.*

I smile. "Well, I am fuucked up!"

Both girls bust up laughing grabbing me for a group hug.

"Good! You need to be wasted this whole trip." Izzy beams.

"Now get back up there and play some music. I'm fine," I try to explain to her, feeling bad she left the booth.

"Girl, I'm done. It's time to party." Izzy bounces from foot to foot.

"Sweet Jesus," Gus says from behind us girls.

———

By the end of the night, I'm smashed. I don't think any of us girls have left this area all night but twice to pee. Seriously, I don't know if it's my first weekend being legally separated and feeling that freedom but I can't stop looking, there are some seriously hot men here tonight. I feel like a slut with all my dirty little thoughts like in this moment, I know Shy's Ginger's, but damn he's nice to look at, as he walks up placing himself in front of all of us, with his hands on his hips and smiles.

Before I can stop myself, I blurt out, "Fuck. Do y'all breed bad boys or something, 'cause there are *hella* fine ass men here." I try to point at Shy but end up swinging my arm around the room pointing at everything. The girls just keep laughing, since that's all we've been doing tonight.

Shy clears his throat trying to get our attention, but I just stare at him while continuing the conversation in my head, ignoring whatever he's saying.

He really is good looking. I shift in my chair until my eyes land on some other hot guy. *See, that dude is hot-as-fuck.* I tilt my head to the side more. *And that dude. Seriously there isn't an ugly guy in here.* I lean back and look to my other side where I see Gus standing. *Oh yeah, Gus' fine ass. He's fur sures a hottie.* Gus looks my direction and gives me a nod. He probably is trying to figure out why I'm creepily staring at him. So, I wave like a dumb fuck and say, "Hiye."

Everyone gets quiet and turns to look at who I just waved and said hi to. Gus busts up laughing. Damn, that is the first time I've seen him laugh, like really laugh. *See he is fine as fuck.*

"That's fine ,we can ride with you, whatever Gus wants to do since he's in charge of us," Izzy replies gingerly.

I look around confused to who Izzy is talking to. Wait, what? Where's Quick? My head starts spinning from moving my head around too much. I look behind me to see if Quick was sneaking around, but he's nowhere to be found. I try to speak, but I'm so drunk the only words that come out coherent are, "Quick. Stuff. Is he?"

Everyone laughs but Izzy replies, "Probably with some barfly. Don't you worry we got it all under control."

CHAPTER FOUR

My head.

Jesus Christ who let me drink so much.

Mary Mother of Jesus, my head hurts! I hate my life. Sleep. Yes, sleep.

I feel around the bed then I feel myself, letting out an exhale of relief when I feel I'm fully clothed and alone. My head pounds and I groan.

"Rise and shine, Ruby Rube," Izzy says all chipper.

I groan again holding my head. "Go away."

"Sorry, no can do. Let's get going. I have places to be, and you have people to meet. Let's go."

I don't understand, people to meet?

"What?" I murmur.

"I have to head into the office, and I want you to meet a few people. One, being my boss and the owner of Spin It, Luc Mancini. Two, I have a surprise for you, that I'm hoping you will like. I want you to keep your mind open to new things today. Like a new future for you if you want it. "

I peek out from under the covers noticing we're in a really

nice room. Izzy is standing next to the bed with her hands on her hips.

"Where are we?" I grumble.

"We're at the hotel where most of Spin It's employees and my security team live. Ginger lives in this building, well, when she isn't at the clubhouse. Gus lives here too along with most of the security team, Alex, and her parents. We're in one of the suites they reserve for out of town DJs. I've stayed here many times during the craziness. Gus needed to come home, so we just stayed here, and it had two bedrooms."

Wait. Did he stay here too?

I look around the bed and see I'm the only one who slept in the bed. I peer up at her with one eye open.

"Where did you sleep last night?"

She turns to leave with a huge smile on her face. "In the other room silly."

Uh-huh. Right.

I smile calling out after her. "Where did Gus sleep last night?"

No reply.

That's what I thought. They're fucking. I knew it! That little slut didn't tell me.

Once I trust myself not to throw up, I move to get out of the most amazing bed ever, and I notice my stuff is laying on the dresser. I look in the mirror and almost scream at my reflection.

Oh, God. What if Quick is out there. He can't see me like this. Shit, how did I get into bed last night?

I look down at my cami and boy shorts.

Who the fuck changed me?

Before I can begin to have a panic attack, my head starts having a pulse of its own, distracting me from my thoughts. I clean up as much as I can and try to look somewhat presentable before heading out in search of coffee and answers.

Once I reach what looks to be the living room and kitchen I realize we are alone. Unless Gus is in the shower with her, we are alone.

Thank fucking God.

I don't think I could handle small chat with anyone right now. I move towards the coffee maker thanking the gods there is some already made. Halfway through my coffee, Izzy emerges from her room all showered and clean.

"You're up."

"Shhhh. You don't have to talk so loud," I whisper.

"You good? Are you going to be able to make it this whole weekend?" Izzy says sarcastically with a laugh.

I look up feeling nauseous. "God, I hope so. I'm not used to partying since Bella was born."

"You'll be fine." She turns to go back into the room she stayed in, but I stop her.

"Are you alone in there or do I need to close my eyes when I come in?"

Izzy turns slightly to look over her shoulder at me. "It's only me." She smiles. "Now."

Sneaky little bitch.

I fucking love it. Shit, I wish I had got some. I need to get laid, but I guess it was a good thing I didn't because I would want to remember it. It's been months, ever since it all went bad with Brody.

Don't think about it. Get up. Get ready. It's my time.

I push my chair back thinking I need to put my big girl panties on and start my morning pep talk.

It's going to be a great day!

———

Three hours later we're sitting in a studio listening to Izzy's music. I was introduced to Luc Mancini, the owner of Spin It Inc., right when we arrived. Izzy has spoken of him so much I feel like I know him but one thing she didn't tell me is how good looking he is and about his accent. Jesus, I love accents. And then when his wife Mia came in, I could see why Izzy thinks of them as family. Mia's so sweet and motherly. I felt right at home with her.

After meeting with them, we headed up to a studio so Izzy could work on some music. We talked about Alexandria, who is Luc's daughter, and Maddox, her boyfriend, being on tour with another couple that DJs called X-Ray.

"Being in the studio, does it make you miss it? Does it bring back memories? I'm sure you went with Brody a lot of the times when he was recording at the label company," Izzy asks while playing with some switches but not making eye contact.

Just get it over with and tell her everything. I take a deep breath.

"Once you left I went everywhere with him. I became the bands so-called manager."

Izzy turns her head to face me. "You have *always* been their manager. If it wasn't for you, they wouldn't have gotten half of the gigs they did back in the day. I've always told you that," Izzy exclaims.

I smile, ignoring her comment and keep going.

"I know you know all of this but let me get it out." I pause. "Brody's a huge manipulator, or really he's a verbal abuser."

Izzy grabs her chest in shock."No. Way. Not Brody."

I laugh. "Will you let me finish?"

She throws her hand in the air making a 'carry-on' gesture.

"He got in my head making me feel like I *needed* him. When in actuality *he needed* me more. I enabled him and did everything for him. I put all my time and effort into him and the band once you left."

Izzy crosses her arms, and I can see the tension across her face. She never did like Brody, but I always thought it was because she hated him taking me away from her but in reality, it was because he was an asshole.

"Ruby, I could see that a long time ago, even before I left he was like that. Why do you think Brody and I always fought. He couldn't handle that I would always tell you, '*not*' to do everything he needed you to do. It was all manipulation. I saw how he was controlling you. I couldn't take it."

I nod, understanding now what she saw back then.

"I know, and I'm sorry I didn't listen to you back then. *But,* we were married and like I said once you left things started to change. He started being even more possessive, demanding and just an overall asshole. He knew with you gone I was vulnerable. Little by little he tore me down, to the point I depended on him for everything."

Izzy stands up to pace the room. "I fuckin' hate him. I knew when I would come home he would either schedule something or take you away so we couldn't see each other. The phone calls becoming shorter and shorter. I felt it, but I didn't want to fight with you." She stops to look at me holding her chest. "I knew in my heart Rube that no matter what, you would come back to me. You're too much of a fighter to let someone control you that much. I felt if I gave you space you would finally see that instead of seeing me fight with him."

I lean forward placing my elbows on my knees and run my hands through my tousled hair, knowing again she was right.

I sit back, wiping my face. "You're right. In my heart, I knew I wasn't happy, and then when I got pregnant, it changed everything. Having Isabella changed my life, the way I looked at Brody and my relationship. He started getting more nasty, demanding things for the band, everything was about him."

"Did he ever put his hands on you?" Izzy demanded.

I chuckle. "He tried a couple times, but it didn't go very well. He's more demanding in the sense of needing me than hurting me. He's fixated on me. And having me with him all the time. He was even jealous of Bella after she was born. He manipulates me into thinking I can't live without him and if things go wrong, it's my fault." I stand up to move around the room. "It's fucked up, but I need to be away from him when he finds out about the divorce. He uses sex and passion to manipulate me. I need to get that fire back inside me so I can fight him off and say no."

Izzy interrupts. "What you need is to get laid by someone else."

We both laugh. I turn to Izzy who is now leaning against the soundboard, and I smile. "You know how much of a freak I am and how sex is a major thing for me. Well, he knew that too and used it against me. Every time I would threaten to leave, he would force me to stay with sex and manipulation."

"Ruby, that's called abuse. So what changed? Why leave him now? What happened?" Izzy questions.

She won't think bad of you. Just fucking tell her.

"When you were in LA on tour, he had me come visit him, saying we needed a weekend away. Of course, he had his gig to play at, and the whole band was there, so we weren't actually alone. He just didn't want me in town when you came home. He either tracked my phone or had some kind of device in the house, but he always knew when you and I would talk."

I sit down on the edge of the chair, gripping both of my knees to try and calm my nerves.

"Since Isabella was born, I quit going with him on tour and even stopped going on long weekends. Isabella is the real reason I'm leaving him. I get the love and affection I need from her, and when he isn't around, I finally started finding myself again. Without the band to buff his moods and bullshit, I started to open my eyes. He would never stay away too long without seeing me. He had to make sure he kept his claws in me. He calls every night and talks shit, but each time he would leave it was different. Since he isn't here in person to manipulate me, it's different. It's just verbal abuse, and I know that now. I think I was truly in love with his music because once I stopped traveling with the band and not being around everyone or the music, I fell out of love with him. I truly saw him for who he was, an abusive asshole."

I pause seeing if Izzy wants to say anything but all she does is moves to sit next to me in her chair and when she smiles I continue.

"Long story short I knew something was going on right when I arrived by the way he was acting. But it was after the show he started acting really weird. He was super aggressive with me, having his hands all over me. Never letting me go more than a few feet away. Asking if I've been a good little wife while he's been away. Wanting to know how horny I was for him and just saying some weird shit. I ignored most of it because he would sometimes get like that when he was away from me for long periods of time, or I threaten to leave him.

"I was pretty buzzed from drinking during the show, and we had a huge after-party in the two room suite we shared with his best friend and drummer, Sam. I noticed people taking pills, I knew it was ecstasy, and when Brody insisted we do it, I knew he must have already been on it, and that's why he was being overly touchy. I've done it before with him so it wasn't anything I haven't done before but I just hadn't done it since having Bella. I didn't take it right away but shortly after I gave in and took it. The night went on and..."

Izzy leans forward placing her hand on my arm encouraging me to go on, but her face is stone cold. "What did he do? It's okay. Don't worry about telling me. I got you."

I take a deep breath.

"It all happened so fast I didn't know what to do, but it all felt so good until reality hit me."

I pause.

Just say it.

"Brody invited other people into our bed. A groupie and..."

Izzy's mouth drops open with shock.

"He invited Sam into our bed. I didn't know it was him at first, or at least I tell myself that but..."

When I say Sam's name, Izzy bolts up from the chair, sending it flying back. "That motherfucker. Why would he bring Sam into it? He knows Sam is in love with you."

She stops pacing the room and takes a deep breath. "I'm sorry. It's okay. Just tell me everything. Get it all out."

"At first it was just Sam in the room. Brody blindfolded me, telling me to trust him, so I didn't know who was actually in the room. I was lost in the feeling and rolling balls on ecstasy. Brody guided me on top of Sam. It was when they were both inside me, double penetrating me, that I actually heard Beth come in..."

I close my eyes trying to hold back my feelings, taking a deep breath.

"Everyone was so lost in their own euphoric state, that no one really noticed or said anything. She joined in telling Brody she wanted *more*. Begging to be taken *again*. Once Sam finished, Brody moved me over, flipping me as Sam slipped out from under me. Brody took me even harder, forcing my face into the mattress. That's when I slipped my mask up to see it truly was Sam, and it wasn't my mind playing tricks on me. Sam was fucking Beth bent over the bed, but she kept staring at Brody, asking for more and that she needed *more* from *him*. I came pretty hard, and as I laid there I felt the euphoric high from the drugs and my climax, I looked over and saw Brody fucking Beth. Sam started playing with me, building my climax back up, and at that point, I said fuck it- flipped over onto my back and let Sam fuck me, it was so good, I called out his name the whole time, letting everyone in the room know, I knew who was fucking me until we passed out. When I woke up, it was just Brody and I in bed."

I push my shoulders back proud and take a deep breath. "At first I thought maybe it was a dream, but my body had reality crashing in real fast. I got up out of bed and left him sleeping. I jumped on a plane and came back home, and that's when I told him it was over."

Izzy's mouth is open, and shock still spread across her face.

Silence.

I sit back relieved I said it out loud. "Yep."

"Holy. Fuckin'. Shit," Izzy exclaims.

I laugh. "Yeah. He, of course, flew home and tried to turn everything around on me, saying that I was the one who talked about getting double penetrated. It was me that wanted Sam. It was me who enjoyed fucking him. Then he went into the I'm sorry bullshit. It was his fault for letting it happen and that it was the first and only time with Beth... Blah Blah Blah."

Izzy, still in shock, hasn't moved.

"Jesus Christ, Rube." Izzy swallows and blinks a few times.

"I knew he wouldn't leave unless I gave in, so I let him fuck me senseless. Which always made him feel better about himself. I played nice letting him think it was all okay but when he went back on tour, I got all my shit in order and moved out. I told him I moved out and that it was over when I knew he wouldn't be able to fly home for a few months. So, he flipped out and did the next best thing."

"What?" Izzy asks.

"He verbally lashed out at me thinking I would submit, cower back to him but that only made it easier for me to stay gone. This is the first time he's been home since all of this went down. He thinks he'll be able to come home, manipulate me and fuck me into submission." I pause. " Which is why I am here. I'm scared he will, and I want to be stronger before I see him again."

Izzy moves to sit down. "Are you okay? I mean, are you mentally okay with what happened? Has Sam tried to contact you? Jesus, I can't believe he shared you.. *with Sexy Sam.*"

I nod my head with a smile. "I know. It's crazy. Yes, Sam left me a few messages, but I haven't returned any of them."

We both sit there in silence. It's a lot to take in, especially with how possessive Brody has always been over me. Izzy and I have always called Sam, 'Sexy Sam' because he is so sweet and gorgeous. It was always our joke until Brody found out and flipped out. It took me months to get my head around why he shared me with Sam, so I know it will take Izzy a minute.

Izzy starts busting up laughing, throwing herself back into

the chair swiveling it around. "Holy. Fucking. Shit! Ruby Rube got DP'd by Sexy Sam!"

I start laughing along with her tossing my head back against the chair looking up at the ceiling.

Izzy stops twirling around. "*So*, tell me... How was *Sexy Sam?*" she asked wide-eyed.

This bitch. Of all the things to ask.

I feel my face turn red and giggle. "He's got a better body than Brody, that's for sure. And Jesus he can fuck. I was rollin' the whole time but damn it was good."

We both continue to laugh, and that's why she's my sister. No matter what bad things happen, she always brings me to the light. I feel so much lighter already.

It's going to be fine. I'm going to be okay.

CHAPTER FIVE

Leaving the studio, I felt like a different person. Telling Izzy what actually happened was what I needed, it was the best medicine for me. I mean, I know I have a long road ahead of me, but with Izzy by my side, I'm sure I can handle anything. I want, or I should say, I need to do this on my own, but I need to know Izzy is here, ready to catch me if I fall. So far she hasn't disappointed me.

We're stopping by to check on another friend of Izzy's, Eva. Izzy told me she was on tour with the girls in Europe. She is, or was, Alexandria's assistant before Alex became a DJ.

The elevator dings and when the doors open to the floor I hear a squeal.

"That would be Eva." Izzy laughs exiting the elevators.

"IzIz, I've missed you so much," Eva beams.

The girl's as small as me but a bit taller. Shit everyone is taller than my tiny ass.

"Hi Eva, I want you to meet my best friend from back home, Ruby. Ruby, this is our *very* bubbly, *very* energetic friend, Eva," Izzy finishes laughing. Eva is bouncing foot to foot with excitement.

I smile extending my hand. "H-"

I'm cut off when she practically jumps on me, giving me a big hug. "Ruby Tuesday! I heard so much about you. I'm so happy to meet you finally."

Just hearing her call me by the nickname my mother gave me sends shivers down my back.

"Don't call her by that name. Please. We hate it." Izzy's voice comes off stern but she's smiling.

"I'm sorry. I didn't know." She releases me, and I smile, laughing. "Hi."

Eva extends her arms. "Goddamn you're gorgeous. Look at that little body. We need to work on your outfits but hot damn."

Eva keeps checking me out by walking around me. I just stand there smiling.

This girl is loco.

Izzy who's laughing, steps in to save me finally. "Eva, leave her alone, we don't want to overwhelm her on her first day here. So tell me, how is work going with Alex? Do you need any help?"

Eva stops in front of us, and her whole face changes from happy to stressed. "Iz, I am dying here." She drags out each word. "Seriously, I have so many demos, contracts, and tours to set up that I'm fucking going crazy. Like batshit crazy."

She looks between the two of us before landing her sight on Izzy again. "When are you setting up your next tour line up?"

We both are looking at Izzy now.

"I'm taking a break from touring right now. I'm working on a couple of songs and just staying local. I need to get my shit right before I go out again."

Eva takes a step toward her, extending her hand touching Izzy's arms. "Sweetie, I'm sorry about all the drama with Dominic. He seriously has some major issues. I'm just glad he's back home in Russia for a few months and not bothering you anymore."

Shit, I'm such a bad friend. I haven't even asked her about Dominic.

Izzy smiles. "Thank you. It was over with Dominic a long time ago. I'm just glad it's over. I need to be single for a while and work on myself."

Eva smiles, reaching out giving her a hug. "Well, I could use all the help I can get. Seriously they need to hire someone to help me. Someone with *music* experience."

That has my attention and I'm about to ask what kind of music experience when Izzy beats me to it.

Izzy always the mind reader. "What kind of music experience do they need to have? What does the job entail?"

This bitch. I see what she is doing. Look to my new future, uh-huh, right.

Eva walks back to her desk sitting down to fumble through the mass of papers.

"I need someone that has an ear for good music and someone that knows the ins and outs of the club life. How to book's events, sets for DJs, so more or less have management experience but most important has an ear for good music." Eva points to the massive stack of CDs and flash drives sitting there.

"I need to go through all of these and weed out the shitty ones. Anything worth listening to we send up to Luc. I am so tired of listening to shitty music. I need a girls' night." She pouts.

For real? This has to be a joke.

I look over to Izzy and back to Eva. "Is this a joke?" I ask Izzy.

She laughs, ignoring me and walking over to stand in front of Eva's desk. "Well, you're in luck. I'm playing at Club Zero tonight. You should come out and keep Ruby entertained while I play. Gin is coming too. It will be like old times, minus Alex."

I jump when Eva squeals, jumping up from her seat.

Jesus Christ, she's loud.

I clench my heart. She almost gave me a heart attack.

We say our goodbyes and set a time to meet up later. My mind is going a hundred miles a minute thinking about that job. Could I really do it? Move away from the only place that I've ever called home?

The elevator's dings bringing me back to reality. When the doors open, three big motherfuckers are standing in the doorway chatting. When they turn to enter the elevator, I inhale.

Jesus, what the fuck do they feed these guys here in New York.

They're all at least six foot, and for me being five foot'ish, that's one big dude. I see Gus is the last one to enter and Izzy beams when she sees him,while moving closer to me and giving the guys room.

"Iz, what's up, legs?" the first guy that entered says, smiling as he moves closer to me. He has a black long sleeve Hurley shirt with jeans and has the burly caveman look going with an overgrown beard and shaggy hair.

Legs? Do they call Izzy legs?

"Chilling like a villain, what about you? What brings the *Wolfemen* here to Spin?"

The second guy gives Izzy a head nod and moves to the other side of the first guy leaving room for Gus to stand next to Izzy. I watch all the men form a semi-circle around us.

"We're here to get the lowdown for tonight. With most of Luc's guys are out of town, so the MC is helping out with your security tonight."

Security? I look to Izzy for answers.

Izzy folds her arms looking irritated. "Why all the security. I usually just have Gus with me."

Gus grunts, "Iz, let it go."

Izzy turns to him. "Let what go? We haven't had a problem in a few months. Why all the security? Is something going on and you're not telling me?"

Gus says something I think in Irish but can barely hear him.

Izzy's about ready to flip out when dude says, "Iz, it's just for precaution. Club Zero isn't a well-secured club, and fights happen there all the time. We just want to make sure you girls are secure."

Izzy turns her irritation to the guy. "Mac, I get it but don't you have a lounge to run? You don't need to be watching over us all the time."

Mac stands at full height. "My cousin is my number one priority. We'll always watch over her."

Holyshitballs.

This is Ginger's cousin, who co-owns White Wolf Lounge with Shy? Jesus, he's gorgeous - scary as fuck but gorgeous.

Izzy backs down. "I get it. I just want to make sure you're not keeping anything from us."

Mac leans back and turns his attention to me. "So, you must be the firecracker I've been hearing about *all* fucking day?"

Gus nods his head with a chuckle. The other dude smirks, looking at me.

I push my shoulders back and take a step toward Mac. "Are you talking about me? Who called me firecracker?" I snap.

Mac starts laughing. "Well damn, he was right about that but..." He moves back as he proceeds to check me out. "... but the marshmallow thing I don't get. You're tiny as hell." He looks to Gus. "Redman, what's up with the marshmallow thing?"

Quick. The little fucker has been talking shit about me.

I feel my face heat up. Knowing he's been talking about me, has every blood vessel in my body bursting.

"Mac, back the fuck off my girl. She had a parka on last night, and it was like three times her size. Quick was calling her a marshmallow."

The other guy who hasn't spoken starts to laugh.

Izzy turns toward him. "You're awfully quiet over there Dallas."

He puts his hands up. "Hey, I haven't said shit. I'm just here."

Dallas? Really?

"For fuck's sake, who named all you guys?" I blurt out.

Everyone laughs and right at the same time the doors open.

Dallas exits first since he's closest to the doorway but Mac and Gus motion for us to go ahead of them. They both have smirks on their faces while we both look irritated.

Gus grabs Izzy's elbow, slowing her walk so they can talk while Mac moves up next to me. "So what's your real name? Even though Firecracker will probably become your new name around us."

I stop and turn, looking straight at him, placing my hands on my hips, I explain. "I don't like those names. My name is Ruby."

Mac widens his stance making him a bit shorter while crossing his arms over his chest.

Goddamn, these men giants.

Mac tilts his head to the side and states, "Ruby, like Ruby Tuesday?'

"What the fuck. You're the second person to call me that today. No, it's just Ruby." I copy him, crossing my arms over my chest, which in turn makes his eyes leave my face for a beat to check out my chest.

"Well *Ruby*, I think Firecracker is perfect for your spunky little ass. You've got fire in your spirit and that mouth of yours, well let's just say you pop off and I kind of like it."

My body starts to tingle in all the right places. I shift my legs to release the pressure between my legs, letting the skinny jeans Izzy had me put on rub some relief.

"Well, I don't." I turn to walk out the doors but stop and turn back, catching Mac checking out my ass. "Tell Quick to quit talking shit about me."

Mac smiles, taking only two strides to reach me before he's towering over me again. "*Ruby*, I don't think any of us will stop talking about your fine little ass for a while, but I guarantee you *no one* will be talking shit." He lifts his pointer finger up, tapping my nose.

He moves to open the door for me to pass through it and when I do he murmurs. "You're hot as fuck alright."

Motherfucker.

I don't look back but instead just walk straight to the driver who drove us here and climb into the car that's waiting for us.

He quoted what Quick said in the truck yesterday. *Jesus, was Quick really talking about me that much?.* Once I'm in the car behind tinted windows, I turn to look back only to find Mac still staring at the car. He probably knows I am staring right back. He pulls out his cell phone and makes a call still staring like he can see me.

Izzy emerges from the building with Gus on her tail. Izzy doesn't look happy. Gus stops following her when he comes up next to Mac, who's still on the phone. Mac says something to Gus, and he nods his head with a smile but doesn't move. Izzy jumps into the car, slamming the door.

"What's wrong?" I ask still staring out at the boys, who are still staring back at the car.

"These fucking men are barbaric. Like fucking cavemen from back in the day. Like do what they say, or they will throw you over their fucking shoulder and just take you, kind of barbaric," Izzy says in a rant.

Folding her arms, she turns to look outside toward the men, who are still standing there staring at the car. Mac says something else to Gus, and this time Gus moves toward us.

"Is he coming with us?" I ask.

"Fuck no. He'll be by to pick us up later," she states.

At that moment the car takes off leaving the guys standing and staring.

"Well, Mac can throw me anywhere he wants. Damn, he's sexy as sin," I state breathless.

We both bust up laughing.

CHAPTER SIX

"Where's Iz?" Eva yells into my ear.

"She had to go on stage to talk to the sound guy. She'll be right back," I answer while holding my vodka tonic up to my lips. We're in the VIP area at Club Zero, and the place is packed. Eva just arrived bouncing around saying hello to everyone making her way to us.

"Goddamn, Ruby. You look gorgeous tonight," Eva exclaims, turning me around so she can see my full outfit.

I look down and can't believe I let Izzy talk me into wearing this out of the house. I'm in an itsy bitsy teeny weeny, little black dress. I have a small muscularly framed body. My boobs are a good handful but nothing to write home about and a perky butt, that's it. I have on strappy black heels that wrap up my leg. Izzy did my hair down and makeup of course. I drank while she got me ready so I'm feeling pretty fucking good.

I smile. "Thank you. It's all Iz's doing. You look great too."

I've never been good at girl talk. I never really had any real girlfriends. Don't get me wrong, I can talk the talk and walk the walk, but in my real life, I don't bullshit around. I think that is why Ginger and I hit it off so well yesterday because she started talking shit to someone right when we met. It was awesome. It reminded me of me. I'm not really into fashion or anything remotely girlie. Izzy and my aunt were always the girlie girls. I just played along with whatever they wanted me to do.

The VIP area is full of Spin It employees and performers. I mingle around with Eva who introduces me, and I find myself really liking the people and their attitude. It seems like a great company that takes care of their employees.

I don't see any of the Wolfeman here tonight. Gus was the only one that came to pick us up, and he's working security tonight. I felt overwhelmed being introduced to so many people and all the names and faces. I like how everyone knows everyone; it makes me feel a little envious, it was always just the band and me. Yes, I knew promoters and owners of clubs but nothing like this close-knit group.

I stop to watch Izzy on stage getting ready to start her set. Gus is always a few feet away watching. I look around for Eva but don't see her, so I move toward the stage. I step down to leave the VIP area when a hand slides down my backless dress. I swivel around ready to punch whoever is touching me when Mac says, "Firecracker, your fine little ass needs to stay in the VIP area."

Looking up, I freeze. He's dressed in a button-up shirt, nothing like he wore today. He smiles down at me. "Cat got your tongue?"

I recover by looking over my shoulder, then back up at him, and I place my hand on my chest acting surprised. "Oh, I'm sorry, are you talking to me? My name is Ruby."

He tilts his head back with a full belly laugh. "Goddamn,

you're a firecracker alright. Jesus, you make my dick hard, and I haven't even touched you yet."

Yet...Jesus.

I blush at this words. "Can you take me to the stage? I want to watch Izzy DJ."

He just stares down at me, with his beard freshly trimmed, again not like earlier today when he was rough looking. Nope now he's all cleaned up, looking fine as fuck, smiling, showing his pearly whites. I smile back. "Please."

Mac shakes his head but moves to turn me in the direction of the stage. Putting one of his hands between my shoulder blades guiding me through the crowd. Once we're on stage, he lowers his hand but still stays close by because there are a few other DJs and their friends hanging around. I see Izzy standing next to the DJ booth.

"Iz, you ready girl?" I yell.

She turns excited to see me "Oh, thank God. I'm sorry I didn't come back. They fucked up all the cords, and it took forever. I was going to have Gus go get you once I started." She looks over at Gus and glares. "*But,* he won't leave my side until I'm behind the booth."

"Why then? Why not now?" I question.

"No one is allowed behind the booth except the DJ and one other person." She nods her head in Gus's direction. "So *he* feels, I'm safer back there, where no one can get to me."

My heart swells knowing Gus cares so much about her. "Awe, how cute. He cares about you."

"See, that's what we fight about. Is he doing it because it is his job, or does he truly care that much? He's like a fucking caveman when we're in the clubs." Izzy groans in frustration.

"Truly you have to know he likes you. He is *always* with you," I say encouragingly.

"I don't know, but I have to go on. Once I start and this

dude gets off, they will escort them off the stage. Stay here, and we'll have some fun."

Nodding, I do as she says. Standing on stage, I watch all the people on the dance floor. I can see everything from up here. I see Eva in the VIP area working the group of people. Izzy drops her first song, and the crowd seems to know because they go crazy. The dance floor thickens with more people. Izzy is beautiful. You can just see her love for music when she plays. My heart swells with pride and love for this girl. She has her hair braided in funky braids all around her head pinning them up so when she has her headphones on it looks badass. Her mini skirt looks shorter than it is because of her long slender legs.

I feel someone behind me, so I twist to look around, finding Gus and Mac walking up. Gus has a bottle of vodka and Mac has the chasers with the glasses. I turn completely around smiling. "Aw, are you two my waiters for the night? I'm a good tipper I promise." I wink, giggling.

Mac laughs. "Well I'm sure you will be tipping someone tonight. We're just not sure who yet."

Gus chuckles. "Ye are all playing with fire."

Mac hands me a vodka tonic before raising his glass. "Nut up, bitches."

Gus has a water, and I cheers him back.

Izzy motions for me to come stand next to her and when I do, she leans into me. "Seems you have quite a list of admirers already." She looks over her shoulder at Mac.

"Shut up," I say.

"Seriously, there's a line, girl."

I snap my head to Izzy. "What?"

"Well for one, Quick, my boy hasn't stopped talking about you from what I hear. I think he's scared of me though and keeping his distance. To be honest, I can't believe he's letting Mac fuck with him this long."

I turn around to see Mac and Gus watching the crowd on the dance floor.

"So you're saying Quick wants to get with me but won't come near me. And Mac is egging him on by flirting with me?" I ask puzzled.

"Oh, Mac started out wanting to push Quick's buttons, but now that he's gotten to know you, he's in line as well." Izzy laughs, moving to switch songs, leaving me shocked as shit.

There's no way these two gorgeous guys want me. Excitement erupts throughout my body, feeling wanted again is exhilarating.

"Speaking of our little lover boy. You want to see why I love Quick so much? Watch this," Izzy states, lifting her headphones up to mix in a new song.

I turn to look out into the crowd in search of Quick.

I don't see him. Izzy pauses for a second. "Okay, you have to understand this song's our girl's anthem anywhere we go. It's a rule if any of us are DJing when the others arrive we have to play it. It gets us all crazy hyper, and well, Quick has become our ringleader. It's just classic."

I nod my head letting her know I understand, but I'm still looking out into the crowd. I see a big group walking in, mostly men and that's when I see Ginger walking in with Shy.

I turn to Izzy who's bouncing around getting the crowd hyped. Excitement swirls through me, and I start to move to the music, and then I hear, "You're going to love this." I smile knowing the song and can just see Izzy singing this song. It totally is her song. "Bitch, I'm Madonna" by Madonna featuring Nicki Minaj, echoes through the club, and the crowd goes crazy.

Looking out, I see Ginger, who's pointing her finger at Izzy, who's pointing right back at her. Ginger makes her way to the dance floor with about five girls, including Eva in tow. The girls form a circle and start jumping up and down pointing at each other, singing the lyrics to one another.

Izzy bounces next to me singing. She points to me. "Bitch, you're going to have fun tonight."

I laugh, moving to the music watching the girls dance around. When a sick beat hits, the girls start smashing around, and I notice Izzy's doing the same dance. I have to laugh they are so silly and watching the crowd do similar moves I smile, and that's when I see him. Quick's jumping up and down as a hype man does at concerts to get the crowd hyped up. He dances toward the girls who're now clapping in sync with the song. A Nicki Minaj solo drops in, and Quick pounces into the middle of the circle of girls, acting out the words singing to each one of them. He's bouncing around getting hyped, bobbing his head up and down. All the girls start to move in crowding him. They all have their arms up in the air pointing to each other for the last part of the song.

Quick turns, looking up to the stage at Izzy, but when he sees me, he smiles big and starts to mouth the words over and over again, "Who do you think you are?" pointing at me, he throws his head back laughing. My heart skips a beat.

He's spellbinding with his beautiful smile and energy radiating off of him. God, I want to be near him.

My clutch vibrates under my arm, I break eye contact and turn away moving toward the back of the stage only to come face to face with Mac and Gus.

"I need to use the bathroom. Where is it at?" Gus moves first pointing to the bottom of the stairs.

"Use that one. It's for DJs and performers. I'll wait for you."

"It's okay. I'll be right back," I reply.

Gus gives me a 'not going to happen look' so I just walk away, grabbing my phone out of my clutch I see three missed calls from Brody.

Shit. Fuck. Shit.

My first instinct is something happened to Isabella, but I know better. He got home today sometime, and he's pissed off. Isabella should be in bed by now it's almost ten o'clock back home. Which means it's time for him to unleash his fury on me.

I start to panic, pacing around in the bathroom only making my anxiety rise. I start talking out loud to myself freaking out. "I don't know what to do. I need to call him back but what do I say. Jesus Christ. I need to get it together."

I move into a stall and sit down looking at my phone. I say to myself, "I can do this."

He doesn't have control over me. I can do this. He's just a man. I can do this.

I take a deep breath and push call. Brody answers on the first ring. "Where the fuck are you?" he yells in the phone.

I close my eyes and take another deep breath before speaking, "Where's Isabella? Is she okay?"

"Ruby, where the fuck are you? Don't make me ask you again. Are you really in New York like Isabella said?" He is seething. I can feel his anger through the phone.

I push my shoulders back. "Yes, I'm in New York. Is Bella okay? Answer me that."

"Yes, she's okay. She's with my parents. I didn't want her to see me like this or hear us fighting."

My heart relaxes knowing my baby is with his parents and not with him.

"Ruby, get your fucking ass home now. We have shit to discuss. We're not getting a divorce." His voice is softer but still stern.

Tears bubble up in my eyes only to fall once I close them. *Stay strong.*

"Brody, I'm not coming home. It's over. Sign the divorce papers."

"Fuck you. I'm not signing those papers," he screams into the phone. "I will fucking come get your ass if I have to. You're not leaving me. We need to talk about this," Brody growls through the phone.

A knock on the stall door startles me. I didn't even hear anyone come in.

"Ruby, are you okay? It's Gin," Ginger says calmly.

I wipe the tears away and try to sound cheerful, "Yeah, I'll be out in a minute."

Brody screams into the phone, "Who the fuck is that? Is that Izzy? That bitch has always hated me. You go and run to your little friend. You think anyone will want you? You're nothing without me. You think she'll save you, fucking think again. You're not divorcing me. You have twelve hours to get the fuck home, or I'm coming for you." Click.

Brody hung up. I start to cry.

Ginger is now rattling the door. I know she heard everything.

Fuck. I need to go home.

Why did I think he would let me go. I need to go home before this gets any uglier. I had my fun, but I need to go back to my reality. Sobbing into my hands, I try to pull myself together but I can't. I hear a lot of commotion, and suddenly the doors lock pops open, Quick is standing there with a posse of men behind him.

Covering my face to hide my crying eyes, I try to speak, "I'm sorry. I-I just need…"

Quick crouches down placing his hands on my knees. "Ruby."

Ginger speaks from behind all the men. "Okay, guys. As you can see, no one is in here hurting her. Give me some room. I just needed *one* of you to open the door *not* all fucking five of you."

I look up to see Ginger pushing all the men out of her way while Quick reaches up wiping away the makeup that I'm sure has smeared down my face. He lifts my chin until our eyes meet. "Ruby, are you okay? Who was that on the phone?" he asks with such a kind and calm voice.

When I answer I try to look down embarrassed but with Quick's thumb and forefinger holding my chin, I can't look away from him. "My husband," I say in a whisper.

"Your husband. I thought you said in the truck soon-to-be-ex-husband," Quick clarifies.

"He'll never sign the divorce papers."

Quick's jaw clenches. "What do you mean by that?"

Biting my lower lips I try to control myself. I need to stop crying. "I need to catch a flight home."

Simultaneously, Ginger and Quick say, "Fuck. No. You're not."

Ginger, who's standing behind Quick says, "Look, Ruby, I know we don't know each other all that well but sweetie, I will not let you go back to that. I heard your whole conversation. Does he hit you?"

I look to Quick.

"No."

His jaw clenches again, and he stands up motioning for me to stand up. I sit there and stare at both of them dazed.

Quick snaps, "Stand up Ruby. We need to get you cleaned

up." He pulls me up to my feet. "Come on. Either you're going to walk out of here, or you will be thrown over my shoulder. I'm taking you to the clubhouse where it's not so fucking loud, and you can relax. Everyone can meet you there after the club."

"I can't leave Iz. She'll be upset, and I don't want to ruin her night." I plead.

I step around them determined I need to stay until I see my face. There are black streaks down my face, and my eyes are swollen from crying. I gasp.

The door flies open, and Izzy barges in yelling, "Where is she" but stops in her tracks when she sees me standing at the sink.

"Rubes, what happened? Who hurt you?" Her voice is calm, but the look on her face is murderous. She looks around for answers. "Someone better tell me what the fuck is going on?"

I speak up first. "Brody called."

My phone vibrates at that exact moment, and everyone looks down to the lit up phone. Brody's name is flashing across the screen.

Before I can react, Izzy has the phone in her hand answering it. I freeze. Gus moves into the bathroom behind Izzy.

"Brody. It's Izzy."

Pause.

"Yes, she's here with me so calm the fuck down."

Quick is cursing under his breath next to me, but I don't take my eyes off Izzy, who's looking straight at me.

"Brody, look. You need to calm the fuck down. She's not coming home until she is ready AND you calm down."

Pause. I can hear Brody's muffled voice yelling.

"Well, if you want to come here and search for her good

luck but I damn well know you'll never find her. So take this time to calm the fuck down and be with your daughter. Ruby needs some time. I have her phone, and I'm turning it off for a couple days. If there is an emergency, Giselle knows how to get a hold of me. I'm cutting off all communication to her for a couple days. She needs this, and if you can't give her that, then it's a good thing she's divorcing you."

Pause. Silence. Brody's muffled yells.

"Brody, I'm cutting you off there. I don't give a fuck what happened. All I care about is my girl, so I'm going to hang up now so I can be with her. Don't make this harder than it already is, okay?"

Pause.

"Goodbye."

Izzy hangs up the phone and turns it off. She looks up at all of us. "Now. I need to get back up there. I put a small mix on so I could go to the bathroom, but I need to get back." She turns to Quick. "Please take her to the clubhouse or Ginger's. I'll be there in an hour - two at the most."

Ginger steps forward. "I'll go with her too."

Izzy moves to me, giving me a big hug. "I told you I had you this weekend. Nothing is going to happen to you here or when you go home. We got you. Now go relax, have some drinks, and I'll be there as soon as I can."

"Thank you," I whisper.

Izzy turns and walks out of the bathroom with Gus on her heels. The three of us stand there staring at the closed door.

"Jesus Christ, I can't believe that was our Iz," Quick says shocked.

He turns to Ginger, who's on the other side of me and says, "Seriously, who was that. Iz's usually the one falling apart being carried out in shambles but that" —he points to the door— "was fucking unbelievable. She just bossed up."

Ginger, looking just as shocked, starts laughing putting her hand on the counter to steady herself, lifting the other one. "I'm sorry. I know this is not the time to laugh but give me a second."

I look to Quick and then back to Ginger, and we all start to laugh. I'm crying laughing, but we're all laughing when Shy walks into the bathroom.

They're shocked that Izzy just told Brody to fuck off and eat a dick, but that is the girl I've always known.

Ginger grabs my arm, pulling me into a big hug before she turns to her man. "Our girl just made me proud. She just flipped the fuck out on Ruby's ex," she tells Shy before kissing him.

Shy laughs. "I heard. Redman came and told me everything. He's going to be hard the rest of the night."

Quick comes up next to me putting an arm around me, pulling me into his chest, and without a thought, I wrap my arms around his waist hugging him back. "Thank you," I say, muffled against his shirt.

"Ruby, you good?" Shy asked.

I pull my face from Quick's chest and nod my head yes.

Shy barks, "Great, now let's get the fuck out of here. The boys are waiting to follow us."

CHAPTER SEVEN

An hour later, I'm shit faced sitting at the bar watching all the people move around the room. Ginger placed me at the end of the bar which gave us access to see the room and everyone at the bar. The bartender, Maze, is a total sweetheart. My drink hasn't been empty once while being here.

The Wolfeman MC clubhouse is not what I would have pictured a clubhouse looking like. It's a massively tall building from the outside. When you walk through the door, it opens up into a huge warehouse type of room. There were a lot of people mingling around, but I went straight to the bar. It's a long bar against the back wall giving the person who is behind it full view of the room.

Ginger and Quick have been by my side since we got here. I haven't said much, and they've been giving me my space. Ginger has been chatting it up with members or Maze.

"Ruby, you coming to the party here tomorrow?" Maze asks gingerly.

I look up when my name is called and sit there thinking about how to answer that. *Am I going to be here?*

Quick grumbles, "Yes, she's going to be here."

Quick has been quiet since we've gotten here. I look over at him trying to read his face when Maze yells, "Okay, what the fucked happened tonight, because that..." —she points to Quick— "is not okay. He has been short and pissy all night."

Maze leans onto the bar showing us her big tits, looking from Ginger to Quick. "What happened to make you all come here early and him to be so pissy. Give me something because this is stressing me out seeing him all grumpy."

Quick looks up to face Maze, grabbing his beer taking a long swig from it. I'm about to say something when a shout echoes through the room. "Ruby Rube."

Maze pops up off the bar throwing her hands in the air yelling, "Fuck yes, Legs! Iz's in the motherfucking house. Finally, something to liven this place up let's get this pole dance party started."

Izzy. Pole dance.

I'm just happy Izzy is finally here. I smile letting a deep breath out. I feel lighter just knowing she's here. She's like my security blanket now. I hate that I need to have someone but it was her before Brody, and I need her again.

Quick gets up, giving up his seat so Izzy can sit next to me. I turn on my stool watching her bounce over to us saying hello to people on the way. Once she is standing in front of me, she places both hands on her hips with a smile. "Rube, how you doing. Have you worked through what happened or do we need to head home to talk you through the shit that happened tonight?"

Gus and Quick move up behind Izzy waiting to hear my answer. She looks so happy and carefree. I haven't worked this shit out, but I'm not going to let it ruin any more of my time here, so I smile. "I'm good. Maze here has been keeping me completely intoxicated, so I'm feeling pretty fucking awesome."

Izzy beams with joy clapping her hands. "Hell yeah. Maze hook-"

Maze cuts her off shouting from behind us. "Already on it. Lining them up as we speak."

Izzy leans in giving me a big hug. "You sure you're good?" she whispers into my ear where no one can hear. I nod my head reassuring her that I'm okay.

She laughs. "Liar." Giving me a tighter squeeze before letting me go.

"Shots!" Ginger yells besides us.

All of us grab a shot. The girls yell, "Cheers, biatches" followed with the fellas "Nut up, motherfuckers."

Maze is full of smiles picking up all the shot glasses. "Legs, you need to jump on that pole and liven this party up."

"Legs? Iz, you pole dance for them?" I say with a laugh and look around for the pole. "What pole?"

Ginger pipes up, "Iz is the pole dancing queen around here, and that's where she got her nickname Legs."

I lift my drink to my mouth laughing as I look to Izzy. "Really? You haven't told me about any pole dancing."

Izzy laughs. "Well we've both been kind of busy. It helps me relieve some stress."

"Uh-huh," I reply.

Izzy stands up, her face going from sheepish to devilish has me worried. "Actually, I think Ruby needs to show y'all how it's done."

Quick perks up,."You know how to pole dance?" He smiles for the first time since being back.

This bitch is going to get it.

"Did you work at the gym with Izzy back home?" Ginger inquires.

"Gym?" I look to Izzy for answers.

Izzy grabs her drink. "Okay, I have a confession. I didn't

really learn how to pole dance at the gym," she states. "BUT. I did teach some classes there once."

I bust up laughing.

Ginger shouts, "I knew you didn't learn those moves at a fucking gym."

Gus moves to Izzy with a murderous look on his face. "Where'd ya learn?"

Izzy stands her ground playing with the straw in her drink. She looks to me, and I nod my head.

"Well, Ruby moved in with her aunt when she was like ten years old. Her momma was a roadie, name Ruby after the song, 'Ruby Tuesday' by The Rolling Stones, hence why she hates the name."

I snap, "Dude. We don't need to my life story. Just get to the part about my auntie."

"I want to know about your story," a couple of the men say in unison.

Izzy continues, "She lived with her aunt, who's one of the top well known domme in SoCal. She co-owns a strip club, and we used to go and hang out in the back with all the girls. Obviously, Ruby was going there way before me but we kind of hung out there when her auntie would let us."

A voice grunts from behind us, making us all turn to see who walked up. Shy, Mac, Dallas and four huge guys walk up from the back room where they've been all night. Dallas repeats himself, "What's your aunt's name?"

Izzy looks to me again for approval before answering, "Giselle."

I see the look on his face, and that wasn't the name he was looking for, so I follow up with, "Mistress Z but mostly she goes by Madam Zelle. She went by a few different names way back when she was stripping, but once she bought into the club becoming co-owner, she stopped stripping. She's been Mistress Z forever, being in the underground kink world, but once she stopped stripping, she started going by Madam Zelle. But, we know her as Auntie Giselle. She tries to keep her lives completely separate."

Every guy in the place's mouth is wide open, and almost everyone has shut up.

Izzy continues, "I didn't want to say anything because she's very secretive about her two lives. She keeps them separate, never mixing the two. I didn't want to have to explain or lie but since Ruby's here, she, of course, has the right to tell you."

Everyone is quiet.

"So, you know how to dance like Iz? You that good?" Dallas again pipes up asking the question with a huge grin on his face.

"I doubt it. I'm sure she's gotten better than me." I snicker.

"Bullshit!" Izzy exclaims.

"I second that bullshit," Mac yells from behind me.

"Let's see what you got," Quick says, walking up to my side.

I laugh and slam my drink back finishing it. "Maybe tomorrow at the party because right now, I'm so drunk it would be a shit show if I got up there," I choke out.

Everyone starts chattering around us laughing and giving their two cents about me getting up on the pole but it's Quick who has my attention. "So you *are* staying?" he says curiously.

Izzy turns to me waiting for my answer as well. "Yes, I'm going to stay the whole time."

Quick's face lights up. "Now that is the best fucking news I've heard all night."

"Well, fuck me. That's a first," Maze says behind me. "Shots. Let's go."

Five shots later, I can barely keep my eyes open. I'm hammered, exhausted and just need to sleep. Izzy is up dancing around with Ginger.

For the love of God, where do they get the energy.

I yell to get Izzy's attention when she comes over and sits down I say, "I need a bed. I want you to keep having fun, but I'm exhausted from the day and hammered."

Izzy smiles.

"I got her," Quick says from next to me.

Izzy asks, smiling at me, "You good or do you need me to take you home?"

I swivel around in my chair to face Quick. "I need sleep. I'm hammered."

He chuckles reaching out, pulling me to my feet. "I got you. I promise nothing's going to happen to you."

"Do not try anything with her, just take care of her. You got that?" Izzy points her finger at Quick.

Quick nods his head. "I got it."

Walking away with him, I start to hear the catcalls and whistles. Quick flips them off before we turn down the hallway. *Jesus Christ, there are a million rooms.* The hallway is long and has a shit ton of doors.

"Why so many rooms?" I question.

"We gutted the place once we took over and made rooms that go all the way around the building. We needed rooms for when other clubs come or for brothers to use."

"It looks like The Shining. Kind of creepy with all the doors closed," I said moving closer to Quick.

Quick laughs. "Yeah, I guess it is kind of creepy, but they're all empty. We're still under construction."

He points to the end of the hallway. "That's the MC club

room. No one that isn't a member's allowed in there. It's where we do all our club business now." He points to the room next to it. "That's Shy's office and next to that is our club office."

We pass the offices turning right which leads to another long hallway of rooms. "For fuck's sake. How many rooms are there?"

Quick chuckles next to me. "Yeah, most of those aren't finished yet, but they'll be just a standard room."

He stops in front of a steel door. "This is the elevator. Most of us live on the third floor. It's a floor of rooms and a small living area. None of us really kick it up there, but we have our own stuff that's separate from down here."

The door slides open to an enormously wide elevator. "God, you could fit a car in this elevator."

"Yes, you can, and it used to. This building used to be a car dealership," Quick explains.

Quick pushes the third-floor button.

"What's on the second and fourth floor?" I ask, being nosey.

"Fourth is storage for now and second is the party room. It's where the pole is and another bar. If you would have looked up to the right from where you were sitting at the bar, you would have seen the second floor. If there aren't people up there or if you're not looking, you wouldn't have noticed it." Quick replies.

The door opens to a living area with eight doors lining the outer walls. Quick walks up to one of the rooms, unlocking it and he pushes the door open, gesturing me to enter. Walking into the room, I notice everything is like brand new. The king size bed, two night stands, and a dresser. I turn to Quick,. "Who's room is this?"

Dropping his keys onto the dresser, he states, "Mine."

Shit. What have I gotten myself into?

"I thought I was going to sleep in a spare room. I don't want to take your bed away from you. Plus what if you want to bring a girl back up here? I don't want to ruin your night." Standing next to his bed feeling naked with only his enormous sweatshirt that is engulfing me with only my tiny weeny black dress underneath. I'm holding my clutch and strappy shoes for dear life.

Quick, who's moving around the room stops and turns to me. He doesn't look happy. "Here, put this on. They're going to swim on you, but it will be better than that dress. The bathroom is over there. I've never had a girl up here. This is where I sleep, and you haven't ruined my night. The bed's big, and you're completely safe in here with me. I would never leave you in a spare room downstairs. I want to be able to see you and know you're okay."

What the fuck- Never? Why me?

Feeling all kinds of tingles spiral through me, I smile. "You're joking, right? You're one of the biggest players here, and you have *never* had a girl up here?" I fold my arms over my chest challenging him. "Never?"

Quick turns around to the dresser, pulling out another drawer grabbing a pair of sweatpants and moves to the bed to sit down where he removes his boots.

"Never. I've had women downstairs, and I never sleep overnight with them unless it's at their house, but I usually leave before they wake up. This is my room to sleep. Now you best get into that bathroom, or you'll be seeing a whole lot of me." Quick stands up to unbutton his shirt revealing a white t-shirt underneath.

Great, I'm a charity case, and he is just taking care of me.
Our eyes lock.

"Sleep huh, that's all you want... I guess I should be so

lucky that you got stuck babysitting me. Perfect," I reply sarcastically.

A bit hurt that's all he wants from me, I turn to the bathroom breaking our stare. My drunken state of mind has my body wanting more, but my coherent mind is telling me to be good.

"Ruby."

I stop and turn to look at him, just as he's pulling his t-shirt over his head showing me his magnificent upper body. His chest is massively sculpted with firm tight muscles. I blink and swallow the 'Oh, Sweet Baby Jesus. Fuck me now' comment that was about to fly from my lips.

Lord have mercy on me. Please let me have this man.

"It's not *what* I want, but it's what *we* need."

Now I'm just confused. I nod with a smile and scan his body one last time, biting my lip before heading into the bathroom.

Confused as fuck, I just stand there looking at myself. He's just taking care of me like he told Izzy. Fuck, I wonder if this is what Izzy was talking about with Gus. Is this how she feels? Like he's doing his job and not really interested in her?

Well, I only live once, and this is my one weekend, so I just need to ask. Happy with my decision, I take my time getting ready for bed.

Hopefully, not to sleep.

I take a deep breath excited for what is about to happen hopefully, but when I open the door, it's completely black except for the small nightlight on the side of the bed where I guess I am sleeping. Quick's big body is turned on its side away from me showing me he's shirtless but completely asleep.

Well, I guess we are sleeping.

CHAPTER EIGHT

I wake up to heavy breathing on my neck and a pounding headache. A large muscular arm wrapped around my waist trapping me against something very warm and very hard. A groan escapes me when my head starts to pound faster as my mind won't stop racing. I lay there trying to calm my mind and pray for relief.

Quick tightens his grip around my waist pulling me tighter into his enormously hard body. The shirt I have on has ridden up throughout the night exposing my stomach. His touch is so warm it has my body coming unglued.

Holy Shit.

Brody never really liked to cuddle, he was so hot-blooded that he always kept his distance, never really cuddling. It felt good to be in strong arms. I wiggle my ass back trying to get closer. Quick moves his hand up my waist, sliding it under his t-shirt, grabbing a handful of my breast. I bite my lip holding in a moan not wanting him to stop.

"Good morning beautiful," Quick murmurs into my neck, placing a soft kiss on my collarbone.

Oh, God. Does he know who he's sleeping with? How

drunk was he last night? I lay there waiting to see what he says next.

His hand cups my breast taking my nipple between his pointer finger and thumb milking it. My body has its own agenda when my ass involuntary starts to rock back against him.

"Firecracker, you keep making those sounds and moving that tight little ass against my body, well, let's just say I won't have much control over what I'll do."

Lost in the touch of his hands I grab his fingers pinching my nipple, so tight I hiss with pleasure and rock my hips back, meeting his hard cock against my ass.

"Ruby, I'm warning you. I have control but you antagonizing me may push me too far," Quick breathes heavily into my ear.

I need more. Another moan escapes my lips.

Quick nips at my earlobe with a groan.

I want more. I slide my hand behind my ass and grip his cock. I'm surprised when I feel the thick fat head bulging out of his sweatpants.

"Fuck. Yeah." He pumps into my hand a couple times.

I need to forget everything and just feel. I move to my back, grabbing Quick's head, bringing it down for a kiss. He still tastes of whiskey.

Quick grabs my hips rolling us, laying me on top of him. He works himself against my core, making us both moan deep into the kiss. I grab both my hands full of his hair, and I tug him up, kissing him harder to the point our lips may bruise.

Fuck I haven't felt this alive for so long.

I start to dry hump him, feeling his cock slide up and down between my folds, has me tingling.

Quick breaks the kiss breathless. "Ruby, open your eyes," he demands.

I sit up on top of him and keep rocking against his cock, I pull his shirt over my head, keeping my eyes closed.

God, yes. He feels so good that I can't control myself.

Quick moves up to a sitting position, wrapping an arm around my waist, pulling me to his chest, and he uses his free hand to help lift my breast to his mouth to inhale. I instantly wrap my legs around him, placing my hands on his shoulders and drop my head back letting all my hair cascade down my back. My pussy has dampened through his loose boxers. A pop sounds when he releases my breast.

"Jesus Christ. Ruby, look at me." Quick's voice is dripping with desire.

I fling my head forward letting my hair fly around my face, and I open my eyes.

Please don't ruin this. Please don't say no.

I bite my lip praying he doesn't stop. Quick's stormy blue eyes are heated with desire. He licks his lips. "There's my firecracker. I want to make sure you know who you're with right now." He leans in for a quick kiss.

I don't say anything but instead just smile. "I see the fire in your eyes baby but where's that cracker? Nothing to say?" Quick laughs, grabbing both globes of my ass giving them a hard squeeze.

"What do you want me to say?" I sass.

"I want you to tell me what you want? Do you really want this?" Quick says with a devilish smile.

I reply right away and completely serious. "Yes, I want this. You don't do girlfriends, and I don't want anything but this weekend. I want it rough and hard, from what I hear you give it good, so yes, this is what I want."

Quick's face has a questionable look. "You sure you want it rough?"

I place both hands on the sides of his face, slipping them into his shaggy hair before I move to kiss him but yank his head back pulling his hair giving me access to his neck. "If I have to repeat myself every time this might not work." Biting his neck I lick up to his earlobe nipping it.

Quick reaches from behind me, mirroring my action, grabbing a hand full of my hair and pulling back hard, snapping my head back, arching my body back exposing my chest and neck to him. I hiss in a pleasurable pain and moan my approval.

"Firecracker, if only you knew what I've wanted to do to this body of yours." Sliding his free hand down my face, neck, over my breast where he stops to pinch my nipple before cascading down slipping it into the boxers grabbing my ass. "And this fucking hair." He tugs harder. "Goddamn, this wild fucking hair of yours turned me on before I even saw your face." He sucks my neck.

"Yes. Fuck me," I grit out.

Effortlessly he flips over, placing me on my back, kissing me. It becomes all hands on deck with us grabbing each other, trying to get closer. He has his boxers off me in record time, pulling back to rest on his shins and pauses looking down at my now naked body.

Feeling self-conscious I start to move my hands up to cover my tits, but he growls. "Don't you even move. I want to look at every inch of you," he says while moving off the bed, leaving me stark naked. He stands next to the bed gripping his cock over his pants.

Holy shit.

His body is pure sin. His whole upper body is magnificently formed with sculpted muscles. There is not one ounce of fat on him. Not like Brody who had a belly. *Don't think of him...fuck.*

I continue down his chest locking eyes on the V dip, where his hands are now moving up and down, stroking his cock inside his sweatpants. Goddamn, it's so defined it has me wanting to follow that happy little trail.

Quick's bad boy smirk has me feeling warm inside. The way he's devouring my body looking at every inch while stroking his cock has my pussy throbbing. His sweatpants drop down, springing his cock free letting it bounce with joy. I take a deep breath before licking my lips.

For the love of God, that's a massive cock.

"You sure you want this? I'm a lot to take," Quick teases, grabbing a condom from the nightstand.

"Are you sure you're ready for me? I'm a lot to take." I push up onto my elbows, biting my lip, wanting his cock so bad.

"That's my firecracker, now get on your knees, I want that fine ass in the air," Quick growls huskily, rolling the condom down his overly eager cock while moving toward the bed.

I jump onto my hands and knees looking over my shoulder with excitement. Quick moves behind me, grabbing my ass, placing his cock at my entrance.

"Last chance, Rube. You sure you want *all of me*?" he asks one last time.

"Yes, please. Hurry," I purr, needing it. *I want a new memory. Yes. Fuck me.*

Quick grabs my shoulder holding me in place before he starts his assault slamming his cock into my core, a sharp hiss breaks through his clenched teeth. I cry out in pleasurable pain.

"Fuck," he growls. "Your cunt's like a fucking hoover.

So. Tight," Quick breathes hammering my pussy, stretching it to form a sleeve around his cock.

"Yes," I mewl.

Quick grabs both my hips digging his nails into my skin, powering into me, grunting with each thrust.

"Fuck yeah, Rube."

Thrust.

"That's it. Fuck."

Thrust.

"Take all of me."

Thrust. Slap.

I throw my head back. "Yes. Again," I grit out.

Quick starts working me faster, gripping my hair, he fucks me harder, sporadically slapping my ass.

"Goddamn firecracker. Come alive, baby. Let go," Quick huffs, breathless.

Oh, God, his cock feels so goddamn good.

"Harder. Fuck, I'm close," I demand.

"I got you. Come for me." Quick pulls back on my hair harder, arching my body toward him. Grabbing my shoulder with his other hand, Quick pins me from moving, giving him more leverage, as he starts jacking his cock upward with long harder thrusts that go so fucking deep he bottoms out. I cry out with my orgasm as it explodes, rippling through my body.

"Oh, God. Quick. Yes. Y-ess."

Quick slows his thrusts, releasing me to collapse against the bed. "That's it, come all over my cock." After a couple more pumps, he pulls out, flipping my lifeless body over as he lifts my legs up against his chest with my feet dangling over his shoulders. He slides under me pummeling back into my creamy pussy. I lock knees as he hugs my legs against his chest so he can jack his cock in and out of me, fast like a jackrabbit. My tits are bouncing all over, and all you hear is the slapping of our bodies pounding together.

"Firecracker, this pussy of yours is making me delirious, wanting more," he says hoarsely.

I feel another orgasm at the brink of exploding, I grab my tits in each hand and wrench, pulling them, sending a jolt of pain through my body. "Quick. Oh, God..." I shout.

Quick's voice comes out raspy. "Yes." He swallows, taking a breath. "Fuck that cock of mine." Another breath. "Come, Rube."

As he says, "come," I arch my back off the bed screaming through another climax. My body starts to shake, and I see stars on the back of my eyelids. Quick releases my legs, spreading them wide apart. He falls between them, lifting my ass up off the bed as he rams my pussy. Sweat covers our bodies as he fucks me ravenously mad with deep and hard thrusts - hitting my clit with each thrust and I come again. Quick quickens his pumps, and I feel his cock pulse, I know he's close.

"Fuck me good. Yes, come hard baby," I coo, watching his muscles pulse and tighten up, as he's about to lose it.

I hold onto my tits, gripping them as he pounds into me, making carnal animalistic sounds. He's close to exploding.

"Your pussy's like crack. I can't stop," he growls through a clenched jaw.

I contract my muscles around his cock.

"Oh, Ruby. That's it. Fucking milk my cock."

My pussy spasms again with another orgasm, sending us both over the edge. Quick lets a long throaty moan escape, and he slows his hips, letting his orgasm wash through him.

"Jesus Christ, that was unfuckingbelieveable." His voice is raspy from being out of breath.

I can't speak but instead moan. Leaning down, he kisses

me slow and deep before pulling out, grabbing the condom, and heading to the bathroom.

I can't move. I can't speak. My body feels like it's floating high from coming so many times, I just lay there.

Quick comes back pulling me onto his chest, snuggling me into him, he covers us with a sheet. My body's tingling all over, I can't move.

Quick swipes my hair over my shoulder, caressing me. "I got you. Sleep. It's still early." I fall asleep before he finishes his sentence.

Waking up again in Quick's arms, I smile. Feeling my body's soreness already I try to stretch out, but I don't want to wake him. He moans from behind me but doesn't wake, instead, he shifts onto his back throwing an arm over his face. I lift up onto my elbow and look down at his beautiful body.

Don't get attached. This was a one-night fling. I try to tell myself that it was a one night stand but I feel a tug in my stomach. Taking a deep breath, I slip out of bed and grab all my stuff, slipping on his boxers and t-shirt again. Opening his door, I stop to take one more glance at his glorious body sleeping so effortlessly.

Goodbye, Quick.

CHAPTER NINE

I feel bad for leaving Quick, but it's the right thing to do.

No attachment. No overnight stays. No drama.

Feeling good about my decision, I push my shoulders back and shut the door. Only to realize that I don't know where Izzy is and where I'm going to go right now. I start to panic making my way over to the elevator. I didn't think this through all the way. Maybe I-

"Goin' somewhere?"

I scream, jumping around to see Gus standing in the small kitchen by the coffee maker. "For fuck's sake, you scared the shit out of me Gus." Clenching my chest, I bend over trying not to laugh.

"Running away I see. You lookin' for Iz?" He grabs his cup of coffee and moves to the table.

I move back toward the table taking a seat across from him. "I wasn't running away. He doesn't do sleepovers, so I did him a favor and left before he woke up," I answer honestly.

"Yes, but what if he wanted ya to stay?" Gus takes a sip of coffee.

Ignoring his question, I ask, "Is there more of that?" motioning toward the coffee maker.

"Yes, let me get it." Gus gets up before I can protest.

"So are ya leavin' today or ya goin' to stay a couple more days?" Gus asks over his shoulder.

"I don't know what to do, honestly. I don't want to go back, but it would make things easier."

"Easier on who? The cunt? What I've heard he's a real prick," Gus says, still not looking at me.

"Who's a prick?" I jump again hearing Izzy's voice bellow from behind me.

"Fuck, is everyone around here ninjas?" I laugh, grabbing my chest again.

Izzy laughs. "I need coffee."

Izzy stops to kiss the top of my head before moving toward Gus who happens to have two cups of coffee. He must have known she was coming out.

"Where's Quick?" Izzy asks, moving toward the fridge.

"Your *one* here snuck out of me lad's room." Gus chuckles. I swoon over his thick accent and his laugh. I think this is the most I've spoken to Gus. It's nice seeing this side of him.

Izzy stands up from bending down in the fridge to look over the door at me. "You left *him* sleeping? You snuck out?"

I shrug my shoulders. "I wanted to find you. Don't we have stuff to do today?"

Izzy shuts the fridge and comes to sit down in front of me. "Um, I don't know how to say this, but he never takes girls home with him." She smiles. "Like ever."

I again shrug my shoulders. "I told him last night it was a no strings attached kind of thing. He agreed."

Gus hands us our coffee, placing creamers and sugar on the table. "Stall the ball, lass. Did he actually agree and confirm what ya just said? I know me, boy, he doesn't take just anyone home. Especially to his room," Gus declares.

"Hello, I'm still married. It's sex. My head isn't ready for anything else," I say simply. I try to convince them or maybe myself that it's just sex.

Shit. I feel bad now.

"Plus, I'm Iz's girl. He's been taking care of me since I got here."

Izzy starts busting up laughing. Gus just looks pissed off.

"What?"

Gus leans forward placing his elbow on to the table. "Lass, your crown needs to be check. That boy doesn't do anythin' he doesn't want to do. I was in charge of watchin' over ya, not him."

"Well, what could he want from me? He doesn't know anything about me, and I'm damaged goods with a shit ton of baggage, and so much drama to deal with. I wouldn't even want to be around me. I can't handle any attachments right now, and I'm sure he doesn't want a headache either. I'm here for the weekend. It's just a good time."

Both Izzy and Gus sit back in their chairs sipping their coffee.

I can't handle any more attachments. He was just some fun I needed to help me forget Brody.

Needing to change the subject I ask, "So what's the plan today and tonight?"

Izzy smiles. "Well we're going to head to my place and get changed and come back. We need to help get ready for the party tonight. I told Ginger I would help her get the food and stock the bar. Plus you need to practice for your dance tonight."

I choke on my coffee. "My dance tonight?"

Gus laughs. "You said ya were goin' to dance for us tonight."

————

We spent most of the day running around with Ginger and Eva getting stuff ready for the party at the clubhouse tonight. Quick occupied my mind all day, which is a good thing considering I called my aunt right when we left the clubhouse this morning. Izzy wouldn't give me my cell phone back, but she let me use hers instead. I called my aunt first to get the low down on what all happened with Brody.

He lost his shit when she handed him the papers. She said she waited until Bella was in her room playing. He went mad crazy trying to get information out of her about where I went. Once he called his parents, she felt better about leaving. She assured me Bella was okay and in good hands.

After I got off the phone with my aunt, I called his folks and spoke to his mom before talking to Bella. Hearing her voice put an instant smile on my face, reminding me why I'm leaving him. She told me her daddy had a meeting but was picking her up today. I cringed, praying he better follow up and not flake. I felt complete after talking to her, getting my love over the phone. His mom reassured me he would be around, and that Bella was going to be fine.

His parents love me and completely understand my reasons why I want out of the marriage. I'm the only reason he speaks to them, which is sad because his parents are great. They actually care about him, and they have supported him all these years. They come from money but are invested in their kids, not like Izzy's parents who only care about money and themselves, which is kind of like Brody, who only cares about his music and himself.

"Got them!" Eva screeches, opening the door. She throws me a packet.

Ginger and Izzy are in the front seat chatting about something, but I've been sitting back here letting my mind wander waiting for Eva to return. She ran into the office for some demos and stuff. We're all going to help her filter through them since she's so behind. When she started talking about the job opening, both Ginger and Izzy chimed in saying I should take it. Eva went crazy loving the idea, so here we are at the label. I had to explain to them I'm not divorced yet and have a life in LA.

"What is this?" I question, leery of opening the package.

"It's your job application." She smiles, closing the door and placing more bags between us.

"My what?" I shout.

Laughs come from the peanut gallery in front while Eva just ignores my yell, moving bags around, situating herself before grabbing her seat belt. "I told Luc you were interested-"

"What the fuck?" I interrupt her. "We just, not even, five minutes ago spoke about this. How did you talk to him already?" I choke out.

"Like I was saying, I told him you still had things to figure out in LA but really wanted the job. He told me to give you the application and that we could work something out if you're qualified," she finished, smiling at me like she didn't just rock my world.

I don't know if I should be mad or excited. It is all happening so fast.

Izzy turns around smiling big, and that's when I know she had something to do with this. I throw the package between Eva and myself, crossing my arms over my chest. "You had something to do with this, didn't you? I don't want any handouts, Iz," I seethe.

Izzy laughs putting her hands up. "Relax, I didn't have anything to do with Luc, but I did tell Eva that my best friend was going through a divorce and was one of the best music managers I knew *and* that she would be here this weekend."

Ginger pipes up next. "Also, the reason why we're saying you should take it is that you can work from LA. Shit, Alex worked from Spain the first few years. It's an amazing job opportunity. Izzy has mentioned you're a great manager and you know your shit. So, I don't see why you're so upset. It's the perfect job for you."

Everyone gets quiet in the car, staring at me, waiting for my response, which makes me cry. The girls all start to try and calm me down, saying it's going to be okay.

I can't believe this. I wipe under my eyes trying to contain my tears. "Is this for real?"

The girls say yes in unison, laughing.

Eva starts rambling about the job, what I need to do while she's foraging through the bags, I reach across grabbing her into a death grip hug. She squeals her high pitch laugh hugging me back. When we pull away from each other, she says softly, "Everything is going to be okay." She pushes my hair away from my face. "You deserve to have the best, and we're here to help you get that."

My heart feels like it's going to explode with all these emotions. I'm not used to people going out of their way for me. Especially people I just met.

Yep, more tears. Fuck. By the time we pull into the clubhouse, my makeup is gone, but I've stopped crying. I'm on cloud nine about the job and all the possibilities it would bring Isabella and me.

We pull into an underground parking garage where there

are rows and rows of motorcycles parked near the double doors. At least I know now where they keep their bikes. I guess since it's winter they don't ride them too much. We pull toward the back of the garage and park next to a loading zone with an elevator where a few prospects are hanging out. They see Ginger and hurry to help unload everything. I found out earlier that Gus is a prospect and not a member yet.

This place is like a hotel even though Quick said it used to be a dealership. This elevator feels like a service elevator, opening to a huge kitchen. "Jesus, this place is huge."

"Yeah, I love it. Before it was a dump and not well taken care of, but we have busted our asses making it what we want." Ginger gleams with pride.

We walk through double doors that open up near the long bar. Fuck, I can't believe I didn't see them the other night. The place is starting to fill up with bikers. Ginger yells when she sees a group of people. I realize all my makeup is probably smeared everywhere, so I excuse myself to the bathroom. Knowing from the night before where it is, I head through the crowd of bikers.

I'm almost to the bathroom door when I hear, "Firecracker. you ready for your dance tonight?" I look up to see Mac, Dallas, and Quick coming out of the office. I smile trying to hide my reaction to seeing Quick. I'm nervous he's mad at me, but I stop in front of the bathroom door and decide to throw them some sass.

"You'll have to wait and see."

The three of them stroll up to me, seeing my face all of their appearances change to defensive. "Why have you been crying?" Quick demands.

Shit. I probably look a mess. I grab my face and rub under my eyes. "I was crying with the girls. It was a happy cry." I giggle embarrassed. "I was just heading to the bathroom to clean up."

Quick steps closer. "Why don't you come with me and you can get cleaned up."

"Thank you, but the girls are waiting for me. We're going to head up to Shy's suite and get ready for the night once we finish setting up the food," I reply with a smile.

"I was going to ask if that was what you were going to wear tonight," Dallas jokes.

"Ha-ha. Funny Dallas." I laugh.

Quick gives them a look, and they both say they'll see me later, leaving us alone. Great, just what I needed. He looks pissed off, and I don't want him mad at me, so I smile and ask him how his day was, like a dumb ass.

He crossed his arms over his chest showing off his biceps. He's wearing a white t-shirt under his MC leather vest that reads Road Captain. Fuck, he looks good. His hair is damp hanging down loose around his face, and goatee is freshly trimmed. "I was worried about you this morning when I woke up to an empty bed. I looked all over for you. I texted Iz asking about you." His voice coming off smooth and calm.

I lean against the door frame. "Yeah, she told me. I'm sorry I left. I just know you don't do overnights and I didn't want it to be-"

"What the fuck? That's why you left?" He cuts me off. "I wouldn't have brought you up to my bedroom if I didn't want you to stay with me. I would have taken you to one of these rooms and stayed with you if I didn't want you. I told you that."

"Um, no, you didn't. You told me you don't do overnights and you have never brought anyone up there, but it's only a few months since you've moved in," I snap back.

Quick's face reddens, closing the distance, he pins me to

the wall. "I told you, that's what I do with the other women. I thought telling you would make you feel special, knowing I don't bring anyone up to my room. You're different. I want you in my bed all night," he grits through a clenched jaw.

Jesus, my body is on fire with him being this close to me. I want to touch him so bad. I bite my lower lip, closing my eyes, taking a deep breath. *Hold it together.*

"If you don't want me, just say it," he drawls sexily. Knowing damn well what he's doing to my body. I place my hands on his chest under his vest. A hiss escapes his mouth. "Fuck baby. Come upstairs with me. I need to get my fix. You make me fucking crazy."

Quick leans down kissing my neck pressing his erection into my body. I moan, gripping his shirt. "I can't. I need to get cleaned up and help the girls," I whine.

Quick bends down grabbing the globes of my ass picking me up. As I wrap my legs around his waist, he pushes the bathroom door open. Once it swings shut, he slams me up against it, locking it.

"I need to be inside of you," he groans into my ear sucking my earlobe.

"Fuck," I moan.

Quick crashes his lips to mine, assaulting my mouth with his tongue. Pinning me up against the door with his body, he slides a hand down unzipping his pants before grabbing my leggings. He almost rips them as he stretches them down over my ass as far as he can, far enough that he can slip fingers into my wet pussy. "Jesus Christ. All I could do today is think of this tight little cunt of yours."

A foil wrapper falls to the ground seconds before he slams hard into me with a long throaty groan. My head hits the door with force the first couple thrusts.

"Fuck yes! Harder," I beg.

Quick grips my ass cheeks so hard that his fingernails dig into my skin when he starts hammering up into me faster.

"Firecracker. I need to hear you, baby," he grunts.

"Jesus. Your cock. Fuck. Yes," I grit out, holding him tight around his neck.

"I'm going to spank this fine little ass of yours later for leaving this morning, but for now this quick little fuck will get us through till tonight when I fuckin' pound that pussy until morning."

"Oh! Fuck. I'm…" I choke.

"Jesus, your sweet little cunt sucks my cock so goddamn tight. Not going to last much longer baby," he says breathlessly.

"So close. Yes, Quick..." I'm right at the tip of coming. Quick slips a hand from my ass cheek over to my asshole slipping the tip of his finger in, I scream out my release, I can't breathe. My whole body comes alive shivering, and my walls contract hard around his cock sending him over right along with me. He curses loud, slamming us against the door a few more times until he slows his thrusts.

I tighten my arms around his neck pulling him to me kissing him slow and deep. His cock twitches inside me making me giggle. Quick pulls out, letting my legs go, standing me up. He smirks. "Fuck me. Firecracker."

I smile, fixing my, now stretched out, leggings. "Fuck me is right. Goddamn, that was giving it good."

Pounding on the door has me jumping. "Quick, you almost done? People have to use the bathroom brother," Dallas yells, laughing. "Brother, there are plenty of rooms."

Quick laughs. "Clean up babe." He leans over kissing me. I move to the sink to wash my face. Quick throws his condom away, coming back to stand behind me wrapping his arms around my waist watching me clean my face.

"Jesus Christ, Ruby. You're so fucking beautiful." Quick groans into my neck biting my collarbone making me giggle.

I laugh at him but don't say anything.

"You good?" he asks seriously. "You're not goin' run again, are you?"

I shrug, feeling sassy. "I don't know." I turn, sauntering by him to the door, and say over my shoulder, "Will you chase me, if I do?"

A devilish smile spreads across his face. "Only if I get to punish that fine little ass of yours."

Damn, this man has me all giddy.

A wicked little smirk spreads across my face as I squint my eyes as if I'm thinking about it. "Hmm, I like the sound of that."

Quick growls, spanking me.

I unlock the door, but Quick moves in front of me opening the door and thank God he did because the hallway was full of people. He pulls me behind him tugging me through the group hand in hand. Well, so much for no attachments.

CHAPTER TEN

After setting up the food, the four of us girls came upstairs to get ready in Shy and Ginger's suite. It's so much bigger than Quick's room. All the other women from Ginger's father's club are getting ready downstairs in the rooms they were set up in for the night.

This lifestyle's so different from what I'm used to. Izzy and Ginger tried to catch me up on most of the important rules. Ones that if I didn't know would get me into a lot of trouble. Shy and his boys are really cool and relaxed, but when all the other clubs are around, they become so serious. Seeing all the guys with their leather vests, which I found out are called cuts, I almost came on the spot. I thought the men were hot before, shit, when they all came out of the club room together, I had a chill run through my body, exploding at my core, leaving me wet. They were that fucking hot. I wanted to jump Quick again.

Ginger is the only one of us not in a dress tonight. She is wearing all leather with her low waist, leather tight pants, a short leather halter top that shows her stomach, knee-high leather boots and lastly, her Wolfeman MC, Property of Shy, leather cut. She looks so fucking badass and independent, making me so envious of her.

The rest of us are wearing dresses. Eva's in a short jean skirt with a strapless top and bootie heels while Izzy and I have a tank top, skin-tight dress with scoop necklines and knee-high leather stilettos. I added a red half cut wool sweater that hangs off my shoulder, but Izzy left hers plain showing her cleavage.

"Cheers, biatches!" Ginger yells. We all repeat her taking our shot.

"Ruby, are you sure you're ready for tonight? If you don't want to dance, you don't have to. There are a lot of people, and you didn't get to practice today," Ginger asks curiously.

"I should be, it's like riding a bike." I laugh.

"When was the last time you've been on a pole?" Izzy asks sounding worried.

I shrug. "I don't remember."

Izzy eyes me knowing I'm lying, but she doesn't know I've been back to pole dancing since having Isabella. After she was born, I'd been on the pole two or three days a week. When I quit traveling with Brody, I started going back to my aunt's place doing at least an hour workout. It is the best full body workout you could ever ask for, and it got my body back into shape, if not better shape, than it was before I had a kid.

I look around at everyone's worried faces and laugh. "Relax, Iz how much have *you* been on the pole lately? Do you remember any of our old moves?"

Izzy faces turns from worried to happy, knowing that if I'm asking that question, that I've been practicing and can hold my own.

"Guurl, hell yeah, I know our moves," Izzy says, gleaming with excitement.

"Oh, my God. I- am- so excited to see you two biatches dance," Eva exclaims.

We make our way down to the other rooms where we meet up with Ginger's Auntie Storm and all her girls from their chapter. The room is packed with girls giggling. I've only met Storm, Sissy, and Gigi but there are four other girls who look like strippers wearing close to nothing. All five of them are wearing three-inch stilettos; they're the only ones not wearing some form of a boot. Storm's dressed like Ginger in leathers with her cut that says Wolfeman MC, Property of Bear. Sissy is wearing jeans, knee-high boots, and a Wolfeman MC tank top. Gigi has the exact same thing on but with a short jean skirt. I laugh thinking we're the knee-high boot posse.

Ready, we all head toward the bar. Once we turn the corner heading down the hall toward the main club area the hallway is packed with people.

"Holy Shit. There are *hella* people here," I say shocked.

The girls all laugh.

"Did she just say *hella*?" Gigi giggles.

"It's a Cali thing," Izzy explains.

Once we hit the main club area, most of the men turn our direction giving us their full attention. I take a deep breath. It's like we're on the menu for the night and they're taking orders. I glance around the room seeing half-naked women walking around rubbing up next to men. More women in leathers standing next to their men taking claim on them and once I see Shy, along with a few others, I feel relief crash through me, knowing we're safe with them. Shy heads our way grabbing Ginger around the waist pulling her in for a deep kiss. Izzy pulls my arm toward the bar with the other girls tailing behind us.

Maze, who is looking beautiful as ever behind the bar, screams when she sees us. "My bitches, finally, you're here."

The men standing at the bar turn to look at who she's talking to, giving us room once they take a look at us, probably hoping we're single.

Maze lines up shots for all of us and once we all have a shot standing in a semi-circle facing the bar, Maze says, "Let's party, biatches." We all salute her. "Cheers, biatches."

Gigi leans over the bar. "Sweetie, let me know if you need any help or need a break. Shy wanted me to let you know I can help if needed."

Maze smiles. "Thank you, we might need some help. I've got two of our girls here from the White Wolf helping because once these ladies head upstairs to dance I'm going with them."

Gigi nods, grabbing her drink Maze just handed her. I hear her say upstairs and I look up seeing the second story is lit up with a strobe light flashing. Music is playing downstairs, so you can't really hear what is playing upstairs, but you can see the pole, so that must be the stage.

Everyone starts to converse with each other while I just stand here looking around at all the different people. It's just so different from where I'm from. I've seen bikers at the bars before but never this many in one place. There must be over a hundred people here easily. Brody played in some biker bars before, but even then there wasn't this many. I see people playing pool, darts and even some older men playing cards and dominos.

"Princess, there you are." Ginger's father, whose name is Wolfe and is the first original president of the Wolfeman, walks up hugging his daughter.

"Hi, Daddy," Ginger says sweetly. While I just stand there and gawk at him. He's seriously good looking. My mouth waters just looking him up and down. I can't believe he's her dad.

"The clubhouse is looking good. I was just telling Shy how much I like the new rooms. It's coming along nicely," he praises.

"Thanks. Shy wanted to make it kind of like how we have it back home but obviously being here we don't have all the space like you do. We're still figuring it out, but so far it's turning out really nice." She looks around admiring the clubhouse.

I look around at the décor and notice all the newly painted walls. I was so wasted the other night and in my own head stressed out about Brody I didn't take in all my surroundings. Today we were working getting things ready in the kitchen that I didn't really stop to admire everything.

Two men walk up behind him, and I swear my mouth drops open.

You have got to be fucking kidding me...

These men are easily six feet if not more and dangerously gorgeous. Damn, my aunt needs to come hang out around here, because these older men are, good God almighty, fine as fuck. I think I've been hanging out at the wrong bars in SoCal. Seriously, I thought LA was where all the beautiful people moved to, but since I've been here, there are mass amounts of hot men, like glorious bad boys, who make your panties wet.

I fan myself trying to keep my face from turning red. I lean back against the bar for support. All the ladies must know them because they all say hello getting a nod in reply. One of them grabs Sissy around the waist pulling her to his side saying something into her ear, making her flush pink.

The other man moves his eyes over me, checking me out

before nodding my direction. "Who's the cute shorty?" I flush instantly.

"She's my best friend from SoCal. Her name's Ruby," Izzy explains.

I can't speak, so I just wave with a corny smile.

"We call her Firecracker though," Mac barks from behind the guys.

I stand up straighter pushing my shoulders back. "You can call me by my name Ruby though." Extending my hand to the big guy with a smile.

"Shorty, if they're calling you Firecracker, I'm sure it's for a good reason, then that's what we'll be calling you." He extends his hand engulfing my tiny one within his. "My name's Cash."

I look to his cut where I see his patch says Vice President. Mac hugs the ladies from the other chapter saying his hellos before standing in front of me.

"Hello, Firecracker. You're looking fine as hell tonight." Mac leans down to hug me like he did all the other girls and I hug him back.

"Hey, Mac." I chuckle into his ear.

"Mac, you best get your hands off my girl before I remove them myself," Quick yells from down the bar.

Mac squeezes me harder lifting me off the ground making me laugh. "Put me down, Mac."

He chuckles. "I love getting under his skin," he says, kissing my cheek.

Quick walks up, grabbing me around the waist, pulling me away from Mac. I look around, and everyone is laughing watching these two fools fight over me.

Ginger's dad speaks up first, "Well, I can see these two fools haven't changed, still fighting over pussy." He chuckles.

"Well we *have* been sharing lately," Mac replies to

Ginger's dad over his shoulder but not taking his eyes off Quick.

I'm sandwiched between the two men, and I can't see Quick's face to know if they're fucking around or being serious.

"Not this one, we don't," Quick replies, dead serious.

Okay, I need to stop this bullshit, so I put my hands on Mac's chest, pushing him back so I can move away from Quick. "For fuck's sake. I'm no one's bitch, so you both need to calm the fuck down."

"Fuckin' Firecracker, alright," Cash bellows from behind Mac.

Izzy steps up next to me. "Alright fellas, leave *my* girl alone."

Mac turns around with a shrug and laughs. Everyone begins chatting amongst themselves with more men showing up to our group. Shy, Gus, and Dallas have joined our little group. Quick still hasn't said a word but has moved to a bar stool behind me. Izzy was swept away when Gus walked up. I just stand there watching everyone laugh and talk shit with each other.

Finishing my vodka tonic, I jingle the ice around using the straw to suck every last drop. I don't want to turn around and face Quick just yet.

"I'm sorry," he murmurs next to my ear sending goosebumps down my body. "When I saw you in his arms…" He pauses letting out a deep breath against my neck. "Fuck, that dress. You look so fucking good - I saw red. I don't want anyone touching you," he explains apologetically.

I'm in shock he is apologizing to me. But fuck, it feels good.

I smile to myself, knowing he can't see me and I love feeling wanted again. He makes me feel so alive and beautiful. Plus, after the men just fought over me, I'm feeling sexy and sassy.

I slowly turn around, reaching over his shoulder, I place my glass on the bar behind him. I purr next to his ear, "I may have fucked you, but remember no one owns me."

Thank God Maze is the best bartender because she hands me another drink. I wink at her as I grab the glass over his shoulder. I lift the glass up to my mouth and use my tongue to guide the straw in, taking a big suck. Quick groans my name low and throaty. I smile, turning away from him and saunter away, leaving him speechless.

Izzy is right there, and I grab her elbow. "Show me the pole," I say loud enough everyone can hear.

"Goddamn, Shorty knows how to dance too?" Cash bellows with a laugh.

Quick barks my name, but I keep walking toward the stairs that I didn't know where there until a little bit ago. I hear all the men making comments when all the girls follow.

"Iz, you best behave. There are other clubs here," Gus demands low, only letting us two hear his plea. He's a prospect. If anyone gets out of hand, he can't challenge anyone unless Shy says it's okay. He has to stay quiet, only doing what Shy says he can do.

"I know. No one will touch either of us. I promise. Shy knows the rules, and he won't let anyone near us," Izzy tries to soothe him with a smile.

"Feck me," Gus groans.

CHAPTER ELEVEN

The second story is full of big lounge chairs and couches that line the walls of the room and a bunch of chairs around the stage. The stage is a fair size with the pole towards the back. Which is a good thing, so no one can reach up and grab us during our set.

One of the girls from Ginger's dad's club is dancing right now. Her name is Lolli, and she's dancing to the song "Lollipop" by Lil Wayne. I start to laugh when I see *she is* actually sucking on a lollipop while doing some floor dancing. The men are all standing next to the stage, some throwing money while others whistle and make catcalls around her.

Our group moves to the back next to the bar. There's an L shaped sectional with a few big lounge chairs. I stand to the side watching Lolli dance, moving toward the pole where she does her walk around, still with her lollipop dangling from her mouth.

The girls move to stand next to me, also watching Lolli. I sense Quick near me, but I don't look around. Instead, I keep my eyes on Lolli. Before long, Quick, Dallas, and a few other guys walk passed us heading toward the bar. I smiled giving him a wink when he looks at me. I love this feeling of having power over someone. I'm usually always walking on eggshells or feeling shitty about myself. Brody would always put me down making himself feel better.

Fuck that! I deserve to feel good. I smile to myself, feeling that jolt of self-esteem come to life inside me.

"Girl, I hope you know what you're doing. That man *has never*, and I mean *never,* settled for one woman. I don't think I've ever seen him with any woman twice. You have him acting like a schoolboy over here following you and shit," Ginger states, chuckling in a low voice.

He makes me have all kinds of feels too.

Lifting my drink, taking another sip. "I told him this is just a weekend fling. I have too much shit on my plate to deal with a new man. *I am* still married, for fuck's sake," I reply mimicking her low voice so only us girls can hear.

Ginger shakes her head. "You must've never been with a biker before, because that man has his sights locked on you and it doesn't look like anything is going to change that, so just don't go fuck around with someone else. It will start a huge fight," she warns me.

I look over at Izzy who has kept her mouth shut but smiles at me and I turn to Ginger. "I don't want anyone else here. Don't get me wrong" —I look around at all the men— "there are some hot motherfuckers here." I turn back to Ginger with a smile. " But I only have eyes for Quick."

I hear Izzy thanking Jesus next to me while Ginger smiles big. "Good. I love Quick, and you two are cute together."

Great, now they're playing matchmaker.

Three performers, two stiff vodka tonics and numerous shots later, I'm itching to be on the stage. I already told Ginger the songs I wanted to dance to and told her to keep them to herself. Izzy doesn't know what I have planned, but I know she will be down for whatever I do. I see the look in Izzy's eyes too, and she loves dancing just as much as I do. It was always something for us to escape to, being able to just let ourselves go and feel the music. She does that when she DJs too, but my only escape is dancing.

"Rube, you ready to do this?" Izzy asks next to me. "Because you're coming up."

I look my best friend in the eyes and I smile, directing a wicked little smile at her. "I'm so totally ready. Just be prepared for the second song when I point to you." I turn back to look at the performer. "Because you'll be in the hot seat."

Izzy squeals next to me. "This is going to be fun. I can't contain myself it's been so long." She rubs her hands together excitedly.

Ginger heads over to the DJ booth and butterflies erupt in my stomach. The room's at full capacity now with men standing around the room with a few in front of the stage. Quick hasn't left his perch next to the bar except to hand me another drink and stealing a kiss here and there but he always returns to the bar. I've kept myself away from most of the men just standing in the back with Eva mostly while Izzy and Ginger bounce around with their men. Maze just got up here and informed me she has an hour before she must be back downstairs at the bar.

Everyone's here, and I'm getting nervous. I haven't performed in front of a crowd besides the girls at my aunt's club or pole classes, in years. Brody always told me I couldn't and that he didn't like me acting like a whore. I called it dancing, but he thought of it as stripping.

Snap out of it. Don't think of that fucker.

Needing some reassurance, I look over at Quick who's

laughing with the boys drinking whiskey. He glances over, and when our eyes meet he gets up and strides over finishing his drink.

Goddamn, he's too good to be true.

I smile. Jesus Christ, he's so fucking hot with his shaggy hair falling around his face. His white t-shirt snug against his chest with his cut hanging just perfect against him, showing off his enormous biceps. I run my hand through my wavy locks, licking my lips when my eyes finally reach his.

"Firecracker, you best quit eye fucking me before I take you around the corner and fuck you senseless," he says, grabbing my waist, pulling me to him.

My body comes alive, wanting more of him, I reach my arms up locking them around his neck pulling him down for a kiss. His enraged cock pushes against his pants in protest.

"Sorry, you're just so fuckin' yummy," I tease sexily, nipping his lower lip.

Quick moans my name, leaning down, he sucks my neck, tonguing up to suck my lobe. "I don't know if I'm going to be able to handle all these motherfuckers watching you dance. And, if you're as good as Dallas says you are, I'm fucked."

Hold up, one minute. What. The. Fuck.

I pull back, breaking our embrace. "What the fuck do you mean, as good as Dallas says? How the fuck does Dallas know how good I am?" I demand.

Quick smiles and before he can answer Ginger's voice booms across the speakers.

"Alright. Alright. Alright…" Ginger sounds like Mathew McConaughey in the movie, "Magic Mike."

"Let's give it up for our girls from the West Virginia Chapter." The crowd erupts when the four girls make their way around the stage. Two of them get snatched up by men throwing them over their shoulder, claiming them with a smack on the ass, which gets more catcalls and whistles from the crowd.

Ginger's voice sounds again. "Okay, now we have a very special guest here, all the way from SoCal. She's best friends with our girl, Legs. And, well, when we found out that she's the reason our Legs knows how to dance we told her she had to dance for us. So, without further ado, please welcome Firecracker to the stage. Remember, club rules, do not touch the dancer at any time during her performance."

I'm pissed at Quick for saying that about Dallas. I search the crowd for Dallas when I see him, our eyes connect, and he smiles big showing me his beautiful white teeth.

Mother. Fucker. But how?

I smile back and make my way to the stage ignoring Quick. Men move, letting me through the mass crowd with whistles, some have words of encouragement, and of course, you have the dirtballs talking shit, which I ignore.

I give Ginger a hug and take off my sweater, which gets more hoots and hollers. I rock my neck back and forth while stretching my arms and I wait for the beat to drop. I've chosen three songs that mean something to me about this weekend. The first one being "Dark Horse" by Katy Perry.

When the first song sounds through the speakers, everyone cries out with their approval. I move seductively around the pole doing a few walkarounds that lead into a few body spirals before I stop, landing in front of the pole, facing the crowd.

Going along with the song, I act like Aphrodite with some Madonna strike a pose moves as I lean back against the pole. I start to slide down into a crouched position spreading my legs wide, showing my lace covered pussy before sliding back up the pole. The men are hypnotized as I snap my hips side to side, extending my arms and snapping my fingers at each side my hip goes to.

I planned on doing a combination of a few really hard drops but need to get my body warmed up with the smaller stuff. I look out to the crowd seeing the girls up at the front of the stage, and I smile. I do a couple of different styles of death drops from the top of the pole, and the crowd's going berserk. My body is humming to the music, becoming one with the pole. Men think it's about sex or being sexy but for me, it about technique, form, strength and overall precision. You must know the song and know when to execute your trick and know what body part goes where and ultimately what move is next.

To end the song, I move all the way to the top of the pole putting myself into an inverted climb locking my knees in a double knee brace. I lower my arms down positioning myself upside down. Hanging there, my tits almost pop out of my dress. I run my hands up and down my body, gripping my tits, I move my hands back up over my face into my hair before I drop, catching myself in a shoulder mount right before hitting the ground.

The room erupts in cheers as the next song mixes in and I lower my body down into the splits. "Don't Cha" by The Pussy Cat Dolls, sounds throughout the room. I bend forward still in the split as I start to crawl toward the crowd, singing the song. Right when I'm next to the edge, I do a couple floor moves. As I'm bent over in front of them, I point to Izzy giving her the cue to head up. I lift my dress seductively until it reaches my head where I rip it off throwing it to the crowd, leaving me in nothing but my very tiny and very see-through matching lace panties and bra.

When I see Izzy standing by the pole, I saunter toward her with a smile. I grab the chair that Ginger had placed on stage moving it next to the pole. As I bend down, I unlock the pole so it can swivel. Most of Quick's chapter members have moved to the stage, placing themselves in the front row. I dance around placing myself behind Izzy and begin to touch her body. I tease her dress up slowly, feeling her body all the way up, ripping it off over her head, tossing it to the crowd hitting Gus in the face. He smiles giving me the 'you better behave' look.

Izzy is a good foot taller than me with her stilettos on, but I turn her to the crowd, bending her over slapping her ass, I slide my hand up and over her ass slipping my middle finger between her ass cheeks giving them a good show. I smack her ass again before turning her around pushing her into the chair.

As I crouch in front of her, and she laughs. "You sneaky little bitch."

I laugh, spreading her legs wide. "What?"

I stand, placing my foot on the chair between her legs, taking a step, so I'm standing up on the chair facing her. I give her a little sexy dance. She leans her head back looking up at me laughing. I twist my arm, gripping the pole, lifting my body into a deadlift twisting my body into a flag while swinging with the pole. Once I clear Izzy's head, I invert into the splits against the pole while the pole makes another circle around Izzy. I climb up the pole doing a few more moves, but each time I pass Izzy's head, I make sure my move is high enough to clear her body. She has her head tilted back looking up at me, but I see her touching herself - giving them all a show as well. Timing it perfectly when I extend out landing back down onto the chair facing the crowd this time.

As the second song ends, I place my hand over my heart and wait for the beat of the last song to sound. When it does, I start to move my hands like it's beating. The song, "Closer" by Nine Inch Nails, has the club crying out again with approval.

I turn around grabbing the pole as I lean my body over her. I start to thrust into Izzy. It looks like I'm fucking her face, but I'm actually telling her what we're going to do next. Placing my hands onto the back of her chair, Izzy reaches up grabbing my tits as I kick myself upward into a handstand on top of the chair. Our heads are next to one another. Izzy reaches up, gripping my arms, and I lean my body back into a backbend clipping the pole with my boot first and then sliding the pole between my legs. Once the pole is secure, I let go of the chair, flipping myself up onto the pole. Izzy gets up, moving the chair away.

I'm almost at the top of the pole when Izzy swirls around below me. We used to do a lot of pole art dancing which is two people using the same pole doing moves in sync or forming ourselves into a crazy design with our bodies.

When I move into a Superman, she knows the routine, and it's like we've never been apart. Each move is precise and detailed. We hear the girls freaking out with excitement. We move in unison, never missing a beat. The last three minutes of the song is instrumental, and toward the end, she grips the pole just below me, and we both slide down the pole on either side landing into the splits, which has the room screaming so loud we can barely hear the end of the song.

Izzy gets up grabbing my hand and hugs me. "I fucking love you girl. You haven't pole danced lately - my ass. That was fucking amazing."

"Well, I had to lose the baby fat somehow," I reply laughing.

We both turn to the crowd and take a bow before walking to the edge of the stage. Ginger's screaming in the mic for everyone to calm down. The girls grab us hugging both of us, but I only have eyes for Quick who has moved to the front of the stage next to Gus. The look on his face is purely carnal, and he's about ready to pounce on his prey as he fingers me to come over to him.

My body's pumped full of adrenalin. I'm still processing what we just did, but my mind is only on Quick. My smile widens, and I feel a huge weight come off my shoulders.

I feel free, and *God, I* am *happy. I can do what I want and be happy. I* am *going to be okay.*

Ginger announces Izzy will be continuing to dance if we could all settle down. I move toward Quick and as soon as I'm in reaching distance he snatches me up, throwing me over his shoulder. I laugh, loving every minute of it. I push up off his ass looking to everyone as we pass. I get a few smacks on the ass. I see Izzy wave and head to the pole for the next song.

I can't stop laughing, knowing where he's taking me, I just relax against his body letting him be the caveman he needs to be. Once we're in the elevator, he sets me down, pinning me up against the wall, smashing his mouth to mine. He's so crazed with lust he's grunting and groaning with one hand grabbing my tit while the other one slips into my panties, finding me ready for him. I grab his cock over his pants, and he breaks the kiss. "Jesus Christ, Ruby. I can't wait." He unzips his pants just as the door dings, opening to his floor.

He grabs my hand, urgently pulling me to his room, still undoing his pants. He lets go of my hand to unlock the door swatting my ass, pushing me into his bedroom.

I turn around ready for him to pounce. He's rolling a condom on, still fully dressed, with his pants open. He pulls me to him pushing me up against the wall.

"Lift your leg up. I want to fuck you in the splits." I move to lift my leg as he grabs my panties, sliding them over, bending his knees so he can place his cock at my wet entrance. He slams into me, rocking me hard against the wall. Quick lifts my leg the rest of the way up onto his chest placing my boot next to his face. He bends down a bit getting a better angle before he thrusts harder, making himself go deeper into me as he leans in.

"Oh, fuck," I cry out.

He has me pinned in the splits against him and the wall as he hammers into me. "Fuck. You're even tighter." He kisses me. "Goddamn. I'm going to come fast." He increases his thrusts.

Reaching between us, Quick slips his fingers between my folds, working my clit.

"Quick…" I grit out.

"Fuck. Yeah," he says breathlessly.

Moans escape me with each thrust of his thick cock as my pussy spasms each time it enters me.

Quick grips my ass. "I. Can't. Hold-" His neck muscles tighten, and his cock pulses, hardening even more with each thrust.

"Harder," I breathe.

"Shit. Yeah. I'm close," he grunts.

Quick leans in, biting my neck. My legs start to quiver, and I chant over and over again, yeah, each time getting louder until my orgasm shatters through me and I cry out his name as I come. Quick growls loud, slamming into me repeatedly before dropping his head back releasing a loud, fuck yes, with his orgasm.

Quick withdraws from me, releasing my leg slowly, he wraps his arms around my waist holding me up. Quick leans heavily against the wall for his own support. We both stand there a few minutes panting breathlessly.

"You've ruined me," Quick mumbles into my ear before kissing my neck.

I reach up, wrapping my arms around his neck pulling him to me, kissing him deep and slow as I drag my fingers through his unruly hair roughly.

Fuck I want more, my body still tingling from his first assault on me, has my body wanting more. I slide my hands down his neck, over his cut, grabbing the sides, slipping it off. Quick stops me, breaking the kiss with a lustful smile.

"Does my little Firecracker want more?"

"Yes, please," I beg.

Quick takes a step back looking me in the eye. "Go lay on the bed. I want you in the splits at the edge of the bed. Facing away from me, leaning onto the bed with your arms straight out above you," he commands in a deep, smooth voice filled with passion.

Without a word, I move toward the bed. My body is primed and ready to go.

"I want those off but keep the boots on." Quick points to my lingerie, licking his lips.

Once I'm in position on the bed, I relax laying forward on the bed, I stretch my arms above my head and place my face into the mattress and take a deep breath in. I just lay there and listen to Quick move around the room silently. I hear him go into the bathroom, probably discarding the condom. I hear clothes being removed and at last, the ripping of a new condom has my pussy twitching in anticipation.

The anticipation is killing me. I love it! I can't remember being this relaxed, and excited, with no worries. I've always wondered what Brody wanted or what he was trying to get from me during sex. These last few years he was always demanding or plotting something while I was sedated and couldn't think straight.

Sensing him behind me, I close my mind off to all Brody thoughts. Quick moves up behind me, but he hasn't touched me yet. I lick my lips eagerly, and my body starts to shake. *For fuck's sake, touch me. Jesus, he's killing me. I love it!*

Quick lightly slides his hand over my ass cheeks igniting a long moan from within me. He massages upward, gripping my side before grazing my side boob and then over my shoulder, only to return back down the middle of my back.

"I know you picked those songs tonight for me. It took me a minute, but I figured it out."

Quick's torturous fingers glide back up over my shoulder, but this time he doesn't return. Instead, he grabs the crevice of my shoulder and neck, putting on pressure immobilizing me. While he slides the other one straight down my ass cheeks slipping two fingers into my pussy.

Fuck. Yes.

I tilt my head to the side releasing a long whiny, yes, while he slowly finger fucks me.

"You got me all strung out over this perfect little pussy of yours." His voice a deep rumble.

He slowly tortures my G-spot. *Jesus Christ, don't stop.*

When Quick withdraws his fingers disturbingly slowly, I protest wiggling my ass.

I whimper, "Please."

He slaps my pussy lips with his cock a couple times sending a zing straight to my core.

"Those songs." He taps my sex, moving his cock in a circular motion. "And goddamn, Firecracker, this pussy." He slowly slides his cock over my swollen clit a couple times. "Rube, what were you trying to say?" He ends his assault sliding his cock up and down my slick folds, coating his cock.

My body is lit up like a motherfucking Christmas tree,

and he wants me to talk. I can't think of anything but wanting his gloriously amazing cock pummeling into me. I clench the bedding above my head burrowing my face, praying for a release. When I don't answer him, he slaps my ass, jolting my face up with a cry.

"What do you want from me, Ruby?" he demands, gripping my ass where he had just slapped it.

"You," I say with a breath.

God, forgive me, but I want him. I want him so fucking bad.

Quick still holding me by the shoulder, leans slighting over my body placing his cock at my entrance.

"Do you want *all of me* or just *my cock*? Because those songs kinda were telling me a bunch of different things."

He continues his torture by circling his cock around my pussy, slipping it slightly in but withdrawing it, teasing me.

Please, don't play mind games. Please.

I get pissed thinking of the games Brody always plays during sex but block the thoughts, pulling myself back to the now, feeling deliriously crazed, I grit out, "I want you. It's only you I want this weekend."

Quick's hand grips me tighter around the neck.

"Please. Quick." I moan.

Don't fu-

Without warning, Quick slams in hard, bottoming his lengthy cock against my cervix. Relief and pain shoot through my lower body. "Yes." I cry out for more.

Quick bends, lowering, gripping my thighs that are still spread out, he begins ramming into me with urgency, grunting, "Only me- Only this weekend..." He slams harder, slapping my ass in rhythm with his thrusts.

I burrow my face back into the bed crying out my pleasure, feeling my orgasm build. Hearing his panting and groans of his own ecstasy sends me spiraling out of control. My legs start to shake from being in the splits for so long but when my pussy starts to spasm, I lose all sense of my limbs. My pussy clenches around his enormously thick cock with my orgasm thrashing through me. I cry out his name, but it's muffled by the bed.

"Goddamn. Firecracker, your pussy-" He cuts himself off slapping my ass.

I'm seeing stars, and my body shakes uncontrollably.

"It's mine," he growls, losing control himself as his thrusts become erratic. "I want you," he grits through a clenched jaw.

I feel his cock thicken with a pulse, so I clench my walls hard around his dick and moan.

"Motherfucker," he hisses.

"Come on, baby. One more time." Quick pushes us up the bed letting my legs slide down, releasing me from the splits but keeping them spread wide. He's leaning over me inches from my body when he grinds deeper and harder a couple times and then holds it there inside me while he slips his hand between the bed and me, sliding it down over my clit.

"Quick," I say breathlessly.

Quick starts to move above me, but it's his fingers that have my attention.

"Oh. Yeah," I cry out.

My pussy gushes with another orgasm. Quick slowly, snail-like slow works his cock in and out. Dragging out his words with each thrust. I'm about to lose my mind, and he's inches from my ear, breathing deeply with each seductive word.

"I'm going-"

Juices slide down my inner thighs. *Oh, fuck yes.*

"-to come-" he breathes heavily, he pumps in.

Fuck, I can't take it.

"-so…" he murmurs, sucking my earlobe with a nip, as he slides out.

I whine, pleading for him to move faster.

"-fucking…" He leans up grinding down harder in and back out.

I'm going to explode.

"-hard." His voice comes out rough behind me as he slams into me, gripping my hips. He starts pumping vigorously hard and faster. He's shouting out words with each thrust but I'm so lost in my own euphoria, I can't understand him. I'm about to have the biggest most powerful orgasm ever.

Hard. Deep. Thrusts. He powers his massive body over me, into me. We both come at the same time crying out our releases.

He thrusts a few more times before withdrawing from me. I'm soaring high as this orgasm has my body humming with electricity tingling from head to toe. I keep moaning, never wanting this feeling to go away. Quick plops down next to me on the bed fully naked, pulling my limp body onto his as he kisses my forehead.

"Rest for a minute," he murmurs raspily.

Oh, my God, again? He's like a goddamn machine. He can't be real.

I can't speak so I whimper.

Quick must read my mind because he laughs. "I mean rest before we head back down to the party. I want you to have some fun with your friends before I take you again, keeping you up here all night."

I relax into him replying only with a happy moan.

I'm stuck. The orgasm has my body humming and with so many amazing feelings rushing throughout my whole body. I don't want to move the ecstasy is beyond anything I've felt, well, felt without drugs. I didn't know I could feel this way, my body is literally floating. All I can do is moan.

Quick still chuckling, thrusts his semi-flaccid cock up against me. "Don't get me wrong, Firecracker. I could keep going."

He turns our bodies so he's halfway on top of me. "...And believe me."

He sucks my tit, releasing it with a pop. "Your pussy."

Quick slips his hand down over my sensitive clit, getting a hissing reaction with arching of my back off the bed.

Oh, my... The pressure. Fuck.

He keeps his torture up, sliding his fingers into my swollen sex. As he leans in to lick my neck, moving up inches away from my ear, he says seductively, "This pussy is going to be so fucking raw by the end of this weekend. You won't be able to forget me." Chills run down my body with excitement. "Just so you know," he finishes.

Yes. God... yeah. I let out a long moan, thrusting my hips against his greedy fingers. Brody never would come more than two times in one night unless he was on drugs, even then it was hard for him. Most of the time he would leave me horny and amped up only to be let down. *Fuck, I want more. I want Quick.* I want to see how many times Quick will come for me. *Come because I made him feel good enough to come.*

He tilts his head so our faces are inches from each other. "Look at me, Ruby," he demands. I obey, opening my fully sated eyes to see lustfully crazed eyes staring back at me. "I want you to remember me and know how much I want you." He grinds his hardening cock against me "I want you again. Goddamn, I want you again."

Quick leans down kissing me deep and hard, crazy like the look in his eyes.

I feel the same way needing him, I reach around his shoulders clawing at him, and he breaks the kiss with a hiss. "Firecracker, if you don't stop, we won't be going back downstairs." His voice comes out rough. His eyes are filled with so many emotions, that I can't read him. I wonder what mine show because right now I want to stay in here all weekend and forget my life. I want him to want me, no I want him to *crave* me!

"Ruby…" My name comes out in a breath, letting me know he's just as torn about leaving here.

A devilish smile spreads across my face. "I can't let you go downstairs with that." I thrust against his fully hard cock. "Now can I? People will think I haven't done my job," I tease.

Quick smiles, moving faster than I was expecting and within seconds, his dick's covered and pushing into my readily swollen pussy.

"Fuck, yeah," we both say in unison.

CHAPTER TWELVE

When we emerge from the elevator, an hour later, the halls are still filled with people. I was having a hard time walking, but the pain only put a bigger smile across my face. I was so blissfully happy I didn't even care where we were or what was going on around me. I have two more days of this dream life, and I wasn't going to let anything hold me back. Not even a broken pussy.

Quick holds me close to him guiding me through the thick crowd. He would stop to shake someone's hand or say hello, but he never let go of me. I was hooked to his hip being introduced to everyone as Firecracker. It made me feel special. He was obviously well liked because everyone seemed to want to talk to him.

The party was in full swing with girls dancing all around giving men lap dances or just dancing around. I didn't see any naked women, but there are some pretty skanky looking ones roaming around. The rooms were filled for sure tonight. We finally made it to the bar where Ginger, Shy, and her family were all hanging out. Most of them were by the bar, but a few of them were playing pool.

Quick had gotten a text from Shy letting him know my dress was outside the door and they would be down at the bar with Maze. I was sad I missed Izzy dance but knew I would see her dance again. We're a few feet away from the bar when I hear the whistles, along with the catcalls and someone says, "Fuck yeah. Firecracker's back."

Quick's face changed from happy to murderous, looking around to see who yelled my nickname. Before we're to our group, I stop dead in my tracks, yanking him back. He was still looking around and was caught off guard.

"Jesus Christ, woman. Don't just stop."

I laugh, placing my hands inside his cut over his massive chest and say, "Please, don't get caveman on me. I told you upstairs I only want you. So, you don't have to worry about me with anyone else. I left an overly protective husband, please don't remind me of what I left."

Quick looks pissed at the mention of my husband, but he takes a deep breath, closing his eyes for a brief minute before wrapping his arms around my waist. "I'm not worried about you. It's the drunk motherfuckers that think any pussy here is their pussy."

I tap his chest with my hands. "I can handle myself. I'll let you know if I can't handle something. Give me the respect to deal with it first. I've been caged for a long time, don't go caveman on me unless I ask you to."

Quick's eyes sparkle with excitement. "Goddamn, Firecracker, I love when you get all bossy." He leans down giving me a quick kiss. "But..."

I lean back breaking our embrace. "There is no but. I can handle myself. Now let's have some fun with our friends." Before he can say anything, I turn and head toward our friends with all eyes on us.

Jesus. Everyone's watching us like were movie stars. Izzy

moves toward me first. "Welcome back, skank," she teases, handing me a drink.

"Fuckoffslut," I cough back, lifting my drink, taking a sip. Izzy just laughs, leaning her shoulder into me giving me a nudge. I fall into place with the girls, and they all tease me about Quick before asking me about how I learned those pole moves. The guys are playing pool, the music is blasting from upstairs, and I'm explaining one of the grips when I feel a hand slide across my ass. There are so many people around us I turn around to see who it was. It could have been just someone walking by and brushed up next to me. There is a group of guys standing in a circle, but I don't notice anyone looking at me, so I turn around. The girls are grabbing our next shot off the bar and as I lean in to grab mine, another hand grabs my ass, and this time it's a full hand grab. I don't make a scene but just grab my shot and turn around, again there is a group of men standing there but not one of them are looking at me.

I look over and see Quick leaning over the pool table taking a shot. I let out a breath, thankful he isn't noticing whoever is doing this and freak out.

What the fuck? Am I really worrying about Quick, I mean, we're not together.

Shaking my head, I laugh.

Izzy says, "What? What's so funny?"

I'm about to answer her, but I feel a hand slip down my ass moving to slide under my very short dress. I move fast and reach back wrenching the hand back, placing him in a defensive move I learned when I was young and have had to use quite a lot being on the road with Brody. Sitting at the bar while my husband was on stage, I've had my run in with drunks before. I turn to face the man that has been assaulting me.

Izzy moves up next to me. "What the fuck?"

The older man flinches but spits out, "Fuckin' bitch. Relax."

I release my hold on his wrist with a smile. "I'm sorry. You must've mistaken me for someone else. Excuse me."

"Goddamn, Firecracker is right. I saw your fine little ass on stage," he says drunkenly.

"Thank you but can you not touch me? I'm actually here with someone." I smile.

Of course, it's a fucking drunk biker. Great.

He's massaging his wrist and doesn't say anything, so I turn back to the girls who are all watching me. I keep smiling. Hopefully, we all can just ignore what just happened. I don't want it to become a big deal. Izzy too has turned back around since I didn't seem too upset but when Ginger's face goes from questioning to angry, and moves toward me, I've already sensed him. I drop down to a defensive position grabbing his arm that was extended out to, I imagine to pull my hair, and I wrench his arm in a twist putting him down to one knee, crying out, "bitch!"

Now people have turned to see what is happening. I take a breath, remembering the rules the girls embedded into my brain all day. I can't disrespect anyone with a patch or cut or something. Fucking biker rules. I look over and sure as shit this motherfucker has a thing that says, Secretary and his name's Sam. Great another fucking Sam in my life. I chuckle to myself. He definitely isn't Sexy Sam, but he's Secretary Sam, like Uncle Sam.

Izzy is standing next to me along with Ginger, and I don't want anyone to get into trouble, so I try again to defuse the situation.

"Yes," I look at the patch with his name again. "Sam. I'm sorry, but like I said, I'm with someone."

The drunk man bellows out in pain. "Bitch, you better let go of my arm."

I see his friends form a circle behind him and one man says, "What the fuck?"

I'm about ready to let him go when Izzy spouts off, "Your man here was groping up my girl. Without consent."

Shy, Quick, and Gus, along with a handful of other men move into the circle.

I smile at Quick who is looking murderously close to killing the dude I'm holding, and the dipshit decides to spout off, "Fuck this bitch. She was fucking showing us her pussy earlier." I wrench his arm harder putting all my weight into it, and he cries out.

Everyone starts yelling at once. The girls are yelling at Sam while Shy tries to calm everyone down. Quick moves to stand next to me and I look up at him with a smile.

He's not happy but when he sees me smiling, his whole body persona changes, and he laughs, folding his arms over his chest. "Well fuck me 'til Tuesday. My little firecracker can take care of herself."

Usually, I hate when people use that phrase but coming out of Quick's delicious mouth I laugh and release the man with a push. I stand up, turning to Quick. "I'll fuck you 'til Sunday, and yes, I told you I can take care of myself. Your secretary here *Uncle* Sam is a little drunk."

Quick gives me a quick kiss before saying, "He's not *our* secretary, Firecracker."

Shit.

Quick's facial expression turns back to enraged when he turns to face the man who touched me. He's grabbing his arm while being helped up by a few of his friends. Shy's talking to the other guys in the group of men while Gus moves the girls back.

Quick faces me again. "What did he do?" he asks concerned.

"He grabbed my ass a couple times. Nothing to fuss over." I smile, hoping he'll let it go.

Quick looks back at the man in question, who is now staring daggers at me, red in the face.

Fucking great! I'm always the problem.

Quick looks back over to me and asks with a smile, "Can I please take care of this for you?"

Swoon. My heart drops. *He just asked me for permission.*

My eyes tear up, but I blink them back. "I'm sorry. I shouldn't have hurt him."

God, it's me. Something always happens to me.

"Whoa...Firecracker. Where'd you go? Come back to me," Quick states as he moves to grab me, but drunk Sam, who is definitely not like my sexy Sam, mouths off. *Whoa, my sexy Sam - where the fuck did that come from?*

"Is that your bitch?" He stands tall bending his arm, moving it around. "How the fuck are we supposed to know whose bitch is whose?"

Ginger mouths off, "you fucking ask them before you violate them motherfucker."

Shy turns giving her a look before turning to the man. "We don't touch any women here or anywhere without their consent."

Fucker keeps yammering digging his hole deeper. "You have club whores. How the fuck are we supposed to know that this bitch who was showing us her pussy earlier-"

Quick moved so fast no one could have stopped him from cutting Sam off by picking him up, slamming him to the ground. His men react, but Mac, Dallas, and all the men swarm around them.

The music has stopped, and everyone has moved to see

what is going on, making it really crowded. I can't take my eyes off Quick. I can't believe how fast he was.

"That bitch is my fucking woman and if you ever call her a fucking bitch, I'll end you, motherfucker."

Everyone stops. I look around. Everyone's eyes are pretty much mimicking mine. Shocked. He just called me his woman.

Shy recovers first. "Quick, let him up."

More people have walked up, and an older gentleman walks up next to Shy and yells, "Sam get the fuck up. What the fuck did you do this time?"

It is at that moment, Quick lets Sam up. "He was grabbing my woman."

There he goes again, his woman. My heart starts to speed up, and I feel flustered.

The man turns to Shy. "Sorry Shy, we have no quarrel. My club means no disrespect and this fucking idiot will be dealt with when we get home. On my word."

Shy just nods his head in acceptance shaking the guy's hand that was extended out.

He turns to the other men in his group. "Where the fuck were all of you? Get his punk ass outta here before he embarrasses us anymore."

The man that I'm assuming is the president of this club, which I can see clearly now that their cuts are different, walks over to Quick, who has moved in front of me and extends his hand out. "Quick, sorry for the problem. Again, no disrespect from our club. I hope your girl's okay."

A few people in the crowd pipe up laughing, but it's one of his men that state. "Shit, Sam got his ass handed to him by the little Firecracker. Quick was just shutting him up."

The old man moves, looking over Quick's shoulder and then down to me and laughs. His face wrinkles up around the eyes when he laughs. He has a bandana wrapped around his head with sunglasses on top. I can't see his patch or name, but when he nods, I smile back.

"Sorry, little Firecracker," he states but doesn't move toward me, showing respect to Quick.

"It was nothing. I'm sorry for hurting him and making it a big deal," I ramble.

Everyone starts to laugh around me and Quick turns pulling me into his side. I see the man's name is Big Pete and he is, indeed the president of the Hellman MC.

Well, hell man. I laugh at all these fucking names. Seriously I wonder where they come up with them.

Big Pete turns to Quick. "She is a firecracker, alright. Good luck, brother." he turns and heads out with the few men that remained with him.

Shy yells, "Shows over, turn the music back on and let's party."

I yell, hoping Maze is behind me and can hear. "Maze, can we have some shots please?" and when she answers,

"You got it, Mama!" I smile.

Ginger is the first one to grab me, but Quick doesn't let go, so she hugs us both. "Goddamn, Firecracker is so your new name. Jesus Christ, now I know where Iz gets it. You're one badass bitch."

Izzy pulls me from Quick's arms and this time he lets me go. She sits me down at the bar, and I'm back in the middle of all the women telling them stories of when I was on the road. The next couple hours is filled with laughs and so many shots I lost count. The place has thinned out some with the altercation, but most of the single men are upstairs where the strippers are still dancing, and I think more of the crazier crew are up there with all the whistles and catcalls.

Quick and the other guys move back over to the pool

table but Quick keeps his eyes on me, staying close. I watch him too, letting him know I'm thinking of him just as much. The closeness these people have for one another and how they had my back has me so overwhelmed. Thank goodness they have moved onto a different subject and now I am just sitting here listening to them talk shit amongst each other. I'm mostly blown away at the fact that not one person blamed me for the incident. That no one said it was something that I did to antagonize him. Sitting here and listen to all the stories. My heart fills with yearning and sadness, knowing I could have had all of this a long time ago if I left him sooner. I feel really happy here and not stressed at all. I get a sharp pain in my chest thinking of Isabella. I miss her so much, but I needed this weekend. I need to be able to confront Brody and move on. I can't even name all the eye openers I've had being away and seeing how my life could actually be without him.

I finish off the rest of my vodka cranberry. Izzy and Ginger went upstairs to handle something with the sound system. Eva left a while ago saying she had a date and the ladies from West Virginia are all chatting about something, so I place my glass on the bar and look over at Maze who's actually staring at me. I smile. She smiles back while making her way over to me, she grabs a bottle of Honey Jack, pouring us both a shot.

"How are you doing girl?" she asks with a smile.

I shrug. "Tired."

"You sure it's tired and not sad? I've been bartending a long time and know the difference." Maze leans over and like always, I look to her cleavage. She has such nice big tits. Jesus, I am drunk.

She waves her hands in front of me. "Hello?" she says with a laugh.

"Sorry, your tits are just so nice and distracting," I say, laughing at myself.

We both take the shot. She's such a nice person, or maybe I'm drunk, or maybe it's because she's a bartender, but I start talking. "I'm just fucked up. I've been in a fucked up marriage from the beginning." My words kind of slur so I sit up straight thinking it will help sober me up. "He verbally abuses me. Like that" —I flick my hand in the air pointing behind me— "thing that happened earlier. He would have blamed me and said it was my fault. See, men used to do that shit to me all the time at the bars or venues where he would be playing, and of course, I would do what I did, defend myself," I say the last part a little loud.

Maze pours us another shot and says, "Fuck that. I was about to jump over the bar and deal with that fucker myself. It was *not* your fault."

I wave my hand at her, "I know. I know. But after so many years of hearing it's my fault I kind of believed it. Anyways, what was I saying?" We both take another shot.

"Oh, yeah. I was saying I hate my life. I've missed my sister. I've missed her so much, but I've been too embarrassed to call her and ask for help." I throw my hand up. "I swear. I tried a few times, but he always sabotaged it. He has cameras in the house, probably in my car, fuck he probably has me bugged. The fucker always knew when I called her."

Maze leans onto the bar again. "That is some stalker shit, Mama."

I flick my hand in the air again. "I know. He wouldn't even let his own band hang out with me. Well, he knew one of them was in love with me... but then, the fucker, let him fuck me! I don't understand that one."

Maze steps back throwing both hands up. "Wait. What the fuck did you just say?"

All the ladies look over, and we both start laughing. Maze pours us another shot and refills my vodka. I sit there giggling, and when the ladies go back to doing what they are doing, she leans in again. "Fuck me. You have to tell me this shit. You can't just drop something like that and not tell me."

I lean into the bar mimicking her. "My husband flew me out to a big event. Gave me ecstasy. Let his best friend double penetrate me and while doing it and had a groupie join in so he could fuck her again while his best friend fucked me!" I say in one long breath before falling back onto my seat.

Maze's face is in complete shock. She looks all around, and I can see she's trying to stay calm. "Give me one second." She turns to walk down the bar and screams, "That motherfucking- piece of shit- rat bastard- cheating whore." All the men down the bar are yelling at her asking her if she is okay. I sit there and laugh.

Exactly how I felt, or I should say do feel.

While she's refilling people's drinks, I look over to check on Quick, and see Izzy and he huddled in a circle behind me. I turn back seeing Maze has refilled everyone's drinks and is on her way back over to me. I tell her right when she walks up, "Exactly."

Maze's face is pure anger, but she calms down some to say, "What did you do?"

I giggle feeling good about myself and what I did. "I snuck out while he was sleeping, flew home and started planning my escape. It's been a little over six months since that happened. I filed for divorce and moved out. He has been on tour and couldn't come home until two days ago."

Maze's eyes are popping out again, and I laugh. "What?"

132 | ANGERA ALLEN

Maze laughs. "You're one tough bitch, girl. You need to leave his ass and move here. We'll become good friends; I can feel it and..." She pauses to lean in close. "Anyone that pussy whips one of my best friends has my loyalty and respect."

I throw my head back. "Pussy whipped who?"

"Me!" booms from behind me.

I jump with a scream. Maze laughs. "See, he even admits it but damn he admitted it today when he announced to the whole fucking place you were his woman!"

I swirl around coming face to face with Quick and Izzy, who both look perplexed. I hiccup, "What's up?"

Maze giggles from behind me and I swirl around again. "What did you do?" I giggle.

Everyone is quiet, and I turn so I can see all of them. Izzy speaks up first. "Quick and I had a disagreement, but it's all good."

Seeing how tense everyone is and that I'm sure I'm missing something, I sit up, pushing my shoulders back. "What the fuck is going on?"

Quick moves closer to me and then we hear Ginger's voice loud over the speaker. "Um, hello bitches, get your asses up here."

Everyone turns to see Ginger hanging over the ledge with the microphone.

One of the ladies says, "Who gave Snow's drunk ass the mic?"

Ginger yells, "Get your ass up here Auntie."

CHAPTER THIRTEEN

Everyone starts to move upstairs to see what the commotion is all about, but Quick tells me to hold on. Izzy moves with him standing directly in front of me. I tell her that if she wants to go up, I'll meet her there, but she just shakes her head letting me know she isn't going anywhere. Concern is etched across her face, while Quick looks pissed off. I want to know what happened.

He leans forward placing his hands on either side of me pinning me against the bar. I smile slipping my hands up around his neck entwining them.

"Hiye!" I say drunkenly.

Quick smiles, touching our foreheads together. "Hi."

Okay, something's seriously wrong. I move my head back trying to see his facial expression. "What's wrong?"

Nothing. From either of them.

I panic. "Did I do something wrong?"

He lifts me up off the chair placing me onto the bar, spreading my legs, which thank God is empty now because I don't have any panties on. He moves in between my legs wrapping his large arms around me, hugging me.

I look down to Izzy hoping for some answers, but she just gives me a nod sitting on the stool next to me. Now I'm really freaking out. I'm naked as a baby down there, and he hugs me. I try to think what has happened since Secretary Sam left but come up empty.

Quick pulls away. "I heard everything you told Maze."

"Oh-kay," I draw out the word, hoping he will elaborate.

"I heard everything about your husband and what he did to you."

I think about everything I told Maze. Maybe he's upset I had a threesome? I don't understand why he's upset with me.

"Why are you upset with me? Is it because I had the threesome?"

Quick steps back. "Fuck no! I'm pissed off at the motherfucker for treating *you* like that and for you to think *I* would ever be mad *at you* for some motherfucker *touching you*."

Relief washes over me, and I smile. "Oh, thank God. I thought you were mad at me? Don't get upset. It's over with, and I'm fine."

"Are you? Will you be okay when you go back?" Izzy asks next to us.

I don't say anything because I start to feel like I'm going to be bombarded with questions.

He moves back between my legs. "It's not over. You still have to go back and deal with that son of a bitch."

Looking between the two of them I answer, "I'll be fine. Being away from him and being here with Izzy" —I point to her before looking down to him— "And you. I want a different life."

"But he's mean, and you've never left him like this before. Are you sure you'll be able to handle it? I should come back with you. I'm not letting you go this time," Izzy announces worried.

"You shouldn't have let her go last time," Quick grits out.

I look between the two of them when a light goes off in my head.

"You two are fighting because of me?"

Neither one of them reply.

"Look. Both of you need to chillax. I will be fine. Izzy knows now I want out and it will all work out." I try to calm them both down. I see Izzy smile, but Quick's still upset. I grab his face with both hands, tilting his head back, and I devour his face with a hard-passionate kiss, wrapping my legs around him.

We hear all the girls screaming, hooting, and hollering from above. I break the kiss and look up to see Mac slinging his shirt around.

"Holy. Shit." I laugh forgetting everything else.

Izzy laughs. "Let's talk about this tomorrow. Tonight is about having fun."

Quick grabs me off the bar carrying me to the stairs. "We have some surprises for you ladies."

Quick sets me down halfway up the stairs, slipping my dress back down into place. We hold hands and make our way into the party room. All the women are sitting around the stage watching Mac stripping to "Just A Little Bit" by 50 Cent, except his mother who's dying of laughter back at the bar taking a shot with her husband Bear.

I pull Quick down so I can talk into this ear. "What's this all about?"

Quick pulls me into his enormously hard body and breathes into my ear. "A few of the guys made some cracks about pole dancing being easy. Some bets were made and obviously lost so since it's just a few of us here now we thought we would give you ladies a little show of our own."

Jealousy rushes through me. "Who do you have a bet with?" I start to think about all the women he's been with, and I get pissed. "Have you slept with every woman here?"

Quick takes a step back looking down at me. I'm sure I look pissed because I'm drunk and don't give a fuck. He studies me looking pissed himself but smiles. "Is my firecracker jealous?"

I cross my arms and huff out, "You *are* the biggest male slut here, I'm sure you've been with all the single girls."

Quick spreads his legs wide, so he's eye level with me, looking me in the eye, he says with a serious tone, "I don't shit where I eat. I have never been with any of our main girls."

I snap back, "Main girls? What the fuck does that even mean?"

"It means I don't fuck around with club girls. I usually get girls from bars or club girls from other clubs but never any of our regular girls. They're like my sisters. It's just something I don't like to do. I haven't had a relationship in over eight years. I fuck 'em and leave 'em until you. You're literally the first woman I've been with twice or in the same week or hell even month. I don't do repeats."

Heart drops. Swoon. *But why?*

"Why me?"

He leans in giving me a quick kiss. "You'll see."

He stands back up pulling me over to a big lounger where Ginger and Izzy sat down.

"I'll be back." And he's gone.

Izzy leans over. "Are you good?"

I smile. "Yeah, just a little drunk and tired."

She gives me a hug. All the ladies are screaming at Mac

pumping his groin up against the pole doing his best impression of a "Magic Mike" scene. When his song ends, Mac stays onstage laughing as he picks the dollar bills up and then I see him… Quick. He jumps on stage, bouncing side to side on the balls of his feet, like he's warming up for a fight. Izzy laughs. "Ah, shit. Here we go."

I look over to the girls. "What?"

"They both love to dance and sing so I'm sure we're in for a treat." Izzy laughs looking over at me. "You remember him at the club bouncing all around. He's fucking crazy."

We both laugh, turning to see what craziness these two come up with and when the beat hits Quick struts out shifting his shoulders forward, moving side to side going along with the beat. "Shake That" by Eminem featuring Nate Dogg. Quick starts lip syncing Eminem's part, acting just like him when Eminem raps, throwing his arms out. Mac throws his shirt back on circling him, acting like Nate Dogg. We're up out of the seats, and I'm on my way to the front. Ginger and Izzy right on my tail. All three of us moving to the beat nodding our heads and shoulders with the music.

Mac starts to sing as he sits down using the same chair Izzy did but straddling it. I laugh when he uses the seat talking about how much ass he gets comparing it to a toilet. He stands up air fucking the chair before letting it drop to the ground and grabbing his dick. Everyone's busting up laughing with these two crazy fuckers.

Quick, who has been circling around Mac, stops and points to me as he raps the song. Quick copies Mac grabbing his package, dancing, telling me to shake my ass. When Shy moves down the stage strutting like a woman shaking his ass, the entire room erupts, everyone is yelling. A few of the men are jumping up and down laughing. He has everyone moving toward the stage up front. There isn't a person sitting, and we all move to the music. I laugh thinking of a scene from "8 Mile" when Eminem is rapping to the crowd. Quick has everyone moving to the beat.

Quick grabs Shy like he's the slut in the song. Shy shakes his ass as Quick grabs him from behind pretending to fuck him. The men act out the song to perfection. Quick moves to stand in front of me hiking his knees up dancing around just like Eminem does bending at the waist.

My heart drops again. This man is killing me. He's so fucking cute. I dance in front of him. Mac jumps down grabbing a girl, bending her over, smacking her ass. Shy stays onstage strutting around still acting like a woman shaking his ass. Quick jumps down and begins gyrating up behind me until the song ends. The club chants Shy's name who takes a bow, laughing as he looks down at Ginger.

Ginger's telling him to get down but Shy looks out to the crowd with a devilish grin when "Down On Me" by Jeremiah featuring 50 Cent, filters through the speakers. Still looking out over the crowd, he points down to Ginger. "I can tell she wants me," he shouts. We all scream jumping up and down. I don't even pay attention to Quick who's still behind me.

Shy dances around singing the song. He takes his shirt off throwing it at Ginger who's ear to ear grinning. *For the love of God, he's stacked.* Jesus Christ, his tattoo on his back is huge. Most of these guys are tatted up but fuck, his is huge. I can't stop watching him. He gets down on the ground, grinding and doing floor moves like Channing Tatum does in the "Magic Mike" movie. Ginger shakes her head, and when he starts to undo his pants she's ready to pounce on stage, but Maze holds her back saying no touching the dancers.

Shy stops undoing his pants, lifting a finger to tsk-tsk us before he thrusts his hips a few times before the song ends. All the guys are throwing money on stage. The whole club's freaking out laughing. My heart is full, and my face hurts from smiling so much. Ginger jumps onto stage and tackles Shy to the floor.

When the next song starts, everyone looks around to see who will be dancing. Quick is still dancing behind me when I hear him say something about Hennessy, and I freeze.

Holy Fuck!

He moves around me, pointing at my smile, and I flush. "Mine" by Bazzi, plays through the speakers. He dry humps the air reminding me of earlier when he took me from behind. Quick keeps circling me singing each word to me. Everyone's watching as they form a circle around us, but I only have eyes for him. When the chorus hits, he grabs me, twirling me around moving his hands up and down my body.

"Goddamn, Firecracker, I want you so fucking bad. Let's not waste any more time baby," he murmurs into my ear while placing my feet on the ground. We start to slow dance as I slip my arms around his neck, his hands gliding up and down my sides as he sings to me.

"This weekend. Ruby, waste this weekend away with me," he says kissing me.

"Yes," I answer, kissing him back.

Grabbing my ass, Quick hikes me up, wrapping my legs around his waist, and we're off again, but this time I know, it will be for the night.

CHAPTER FOURTEEN

Waking up in Quick's arms was the best feeling ever. For once I didn't wake up feeling down, depressed, stressed, or sad. I just felt at peace and sore. He took me so many ways last night I probably won't be able to walk today, much less dance tonight at the club. Izzy is DJing at Club Spin. I'm so excited for tonight. I'll get to chat with Luc tonight about the job they want me to interview for, which I'm still in shock about.

Quick moans next to me as I snuggle in closer, running my hands over his bare chest. He was saying some crazy things last night, so I'm nervous to see what he says today when we're both sober. I leave tomorrow afternoon back to my fuckedup life to sort through my bullshit. I know there's something between us, but I can't even think about the what ifs. He's not going to wait around for me, and I would never ask him to. It could be a year or more before I can actually move here if I move here at all.

God, please let it all work out okay.

Dread starts to wash over me, and I tense up. Quick rubs me, caressing my back up over my shoulder.

"Good morning, I'm glad you didn't run off." His voice's a low rumble waking up.

"Good morning. How can I run when I can barely move," I teased?

"Hmm. And you will be even more sore once I take you again tonight." He shifts us, pushing me to my back and he moves between my legs. I open them willingly and wait, but he doesn't move to take me. Instead, he stares down at me with questioning eyes.

"What?" I ask.

"I feel like we should talk," he replies hesitantly.

No. No. Please. No. Let's not ruin my last day.

My eyes must relay what I'm thinking because he leans down, kissing me.

Quick breaks the kiss. "I want you."

"Take me," I pant.

"No, I mean I want to see you again. I know you have a shit ton of bullshit to deal with back home, but I want to keep talking to you. Hopefully, keep seeing you."

For the love of God, yes. I close my eyes. I can't think that way. This is nice, but it's not real.

"I can't do this right now. I'm still married." I try to get out from under him, but he pins me under him.

"I know that. Believe me, I know, and it kills me you have to go back and deal with that son of a bitch alone."

"My daughter is there, I have to go back." Just mentioning her, I get tears in my eyes. I miss her so much.

Quick drops his head. "I know."

I snap, "Do you? Quick, you have no idea how much I needed this weekend away, but have you thought this through? I have a three-year-old daughter. If I move here, I'll have her full time. No let's go party every night and get drunk.'" I try to explain nicely, but it comes out harsh.

"Look, Ruby, all I'm saying is after tomorrow I want to keep pursuing this" —he waves his hands between us— "whatever this is. I just don't want it to end. Is all I'm trying to say."

"Why?" I hold my breath waiting for the answer.

"Seriously? I was done when I first saw you at the airport. Then when you mouthed off in the truck, I wanted to know everything about you." His eyes sparkle with so much emotion that I had to close mine.

"I don't even know your name. Hell, you don't even know mine," I rant out, frustrated. Fighting how I feel because, in reality, this can't work.

Quick shoots back, "Your name is Ruby Malone. You're one of the Malone duos. You got married six years ago. Your daughter's name is Isabella Malone after Izzy," he replied without hesitation.

Holy shit!

I gasp. "How do you know all of that?"

He closes his eyes, taking a deep breath. "We do a background check on everyone that is close to our members."

I push him, catching him off guard and sit up. "Is that how Dallas knew about my dancing? What else do you know?"

Quick ran his hands through his hair nervously. "Well, after dropping you off at White Wolfe, I had Dallas do a full search on you. I needed to know more about you. I was hooked. I wanted everything."

I scoot back to the headboard pulling the sheets over my naked body.

"Okay, that is some stalker shit. You know that, right? I don't know anything about you. You've been playing me from the beginning?" Sounding hurt and sad, I close my eyes.

Why...

"I haven't been playing you. Fuck, Ruby, I've never caught a feeling this hard before. You've got me acting like a teenager over here. I haven't lied to you about anything. I just didn't tell you about the background check. You can ask anyone, we do a full screen on everyone. I just asked to see it."

"Again. Quick, why me?" I breathed.

He moves closer sitting on his shins fully naked, showing me all his glorious body. "I don't know. I've been trying to figure that out myself. I just saw you, or actually, that hideous fucking jacket, all this beautiful crazy hair and when I saw your eyes for the first time, I was hooked. I wanted to throw you over my shoulder that instant and fuck you in my truck. It took everything I had to leave you there. That's why I came back here and asked to see your file."

"They had the file on me before I even came here?" Sounding shocked.

"Yes, since all this bullshit over the last year or so we do a background check on anyone that even talks to the Spin girls. That included family, friends, and everyone they knew. We needed to be certain you weren't being used to get to one of the girls," he answers honestly.

"I just don't understand. We're lifetime friends."

"Yeah, lifetime friends that haven't spoken but a few times in the last year and all of a sudden you want to come visit and need help."

"Jesus, it does sound bad," I reply, pulling my knees up to my chest. My heart hurts thinking of how bad of a friend I've been. "I've been a bad friend."

"What the fuck are you talking about?" he demands, moving closer, he touches one of my knees. "That's what Iz and I were fighting about last night. I was pissed off and confronted her. Asking her why she didn't try saving you or helping you get away from him. Why she left you with him—"

"I wouldn't leave him," I cut him off. "It wasn't her fault. Everyone tried to warn me, but I didn't care. I felt important, and the band needed me. They all made me feel special. It wasn't just Brody. The whole band was—"

"Neither one of you are at fault," he says interrupting me. "After talking to Izzy and hearing you, I thought about it, and you both were young and did what you thought was best. I see Izzy's side, but I understand your thinking as well." He pauses. "The main thing is that you learned from it and you're getting out of the marriage."

"My life isn't all peaches. I had a pretty hard childhood until I moved in with Brody. Brody came from money and took care of me, gave me what I thought was stability but really it was just lies and manipulation. I'm the reason he has a record deal. I got that for them. I took care of everything."

"What changed?" Quick asks, moving to sit next to me, leaning up against his headboard.

"I had Isabella. I changed. Brody wasn't first anymore, and it drove him nuts. He was always a very jealous man, but instead of him beating the shit out of the other man, he would tell me it was my fault. Switch it around on me. He was just a fucking coward," I answer, hugging my knees, as I place my forehead down on top of them.

Quick puts his hand on my back caressing me, trying to soothe me.

"Well, my name is Jake Reeves, and I'm twenty-seven-years-old."

I tilt my head to the side to look at him. *Jake Reeves...*

I smile. "You don't look like a Jake to me," I say teasing.

"I'm not Jake Reeves anymore. I left him behind when I moved to West Virginia with Shy," he explains.

I lean back, giving him my full attention, hoping he will continue.

Quick grabs the sheet I have covering myself and stretches his legs out under it covering himself beside me. "I've been on my own pretty much since I was of age. I've moved around a lot. I met Shy and the MC about five years ago when I was living down in Myrtle Beach. It was Bike Week, and they were all fucked up partying. Shy wasn't P\president of his club then and was still living back at the original clubhouse in West Virginia under Wolfe, Ginger's father." He pauses obviously thinking back to that day. "Let's just say some stuff went down and I was there for the club. I hung with them for the rest of the week. Before Shy left to head back home, he told me if I ever needed or wanted anything to give him a call."

I've turned my body facing him now waiting for him to continue, when he doesn't I ask, "So what happened? Did you call or go see him?"

Quick laughs. "Obviously, I called him, or I wouldn't be here today?"

"Seriously, you're going to leave me hanging? You just called him one day, that's it?" I say sarcastically.

"I can't tell you the details of what happened, but yes, I called him one day and said, 'hey I need a new life' and bam, here I am. Shy was traveling back and forth from here and West Virginia. I was his main guy he planted here. Ginger didn't know who I was, so it worked perfectly. I wasn't a member. No one really knew me except Shy, Mac, and Dallas." He nudges me. "They even did a background check on me, so don't feel bad."

"Well let me see your file," I snap back.

Quick pulls me onto his lap, and I comply, straddling him. "Look, Ruby... I like you. That's all I know, and I want you to know how I feel. I haven't had anything good in my life until this club and being around Shy all these years hearing him tell me about his love for Ginger. Seeing him struggle and fight for his love for her. Half the time I thought he was nuts until I saw her on stage playing."

Quick paused, closing his eyes, he leaned his head back taking a deep breath. I just sit there watching him, memorizing his beautifully sculpted face.

"See, Shy tells everyone it was not love at first sight, but instead it was her voice. She sounded like an angel, and she saved him. They've been together ever since. His love never faltering. Being around that for almost three years sticks and when I saw that hair of yours something just clicked. I can't explain it and I know I probably sound crazy but damn, Firecracker, you got me. I know it in my gut." He reaches around, grabbing the globes of my ass pulling me down hard against his readily hardened cock. "Then you gave me this divine pussy, and it was a wrap. I don't want anyone else. So, you do what you need to do, and I'll be here for you."

This can't be real.

I have tears in my eyes, and I don't fight them, but instead, I let them fall, just like my heart. Quick reaches up wiping the tears away, gripping my face. "Ruby, baby don't cry." I lean down and brush my lips against his softly. "I'm happy. Thank you for that, you made me happy."

Quick runs his hand through my hair, down my back, over my hips gripping my ass, motioning me to rock against his hard shaft sliding between my slick folds. My swollen pussy stings from the friction, but the pain feels good.

"Ruby. Jesus, you make me feel like a fucking teenage kid, all I want to do is come over and over again." Quick kisses my neck, biting my collarbone.

My head falls back giving him full access to my body.

"Quick, take me." I look back down, letting my hair fall around my face. "Slow and deep," I say, licking my lips, shifting up and back again on his now slick cock.

Quick kisses me reaching around, hugging me to his chest as he thrusts up a few times with his heated cock, now uncovered has me moaning for more.

"Take me now." I look him in the eyes with a begging plea.

"Anything for you."

CHAPTER FIFTEEN

"Rube, we need to have a talk," Izzy says quietly from across her room.

Jesus, another one. Feeling drained from my chat with Quick this morning, I don't know if I can handle another "talk," but she's my best friend, so I turn to her with a smile and say, "Sure, what's up?"

She looks perplexed which puts me on edge. We have been at her place for an hour getting ready for tonight.

"Don't get mad but I turned your phone on this morning and listened to all your voicemails," she says sheepishly.

"Oh-kay, why would that make me mad? We always used to do that, why would it be any different now. I have nothing to hide. I'm sure they're all Brody flipping out. You can just delete them."

I knew nothing was wrong with Bella and that she was okay since I had spoken with her earlier today. She was with my aunt having a great time shopping. So, I don't understand Izzy's facial expression.

"Yeah, they're mostly him flipping out which we'll get to but um…" She pauses. "Sam left a few too."

"Holy shit. What did he say? Where's my phone?" I look around her room where we're getting ready.

Izzy just keeps staring at me. "He wants to be with you. He said a lot, and you probably should listen to it, but I'm nervous."

I move to stand up from off the ground, where I've been straightening my hair and sit on the bed where Izzy has sat down, giving her my full attention. "Why would you be nervous?"

"I don't want you to be with Sam. I want you to move here with me. You can live here with Bella, or we can get a suite at the building Luc owns. I haven't pushed, and I'm trying to be supportive this weekend, but after Quick laid into me, I feel I need to speak up."

When I don't say anything, she keeps going. "These past few days I feel whole again with you here. I feel we both are better together when we're in each other's lives. You give me strength as much as I do you. I want you to move here and do what you want to do, not what some guy wants you to do. That includes Quick. I love him to death and would be over the moon if you dated him, but I want you to do what you want. I want you to do it here with me though."

I have tears in my eyes as I lean over giving her a big hug. "I love you too and feel the same way. I'm going to do what's best for Bella and me. I promise. I pray it works out that I can move here, but I need to go home and deal with my life. No matter what Sam or Quick or even Brody says will keep me from doing right by my baby girl. I needed this weekend to remind me I do have a life without Brody."

She releases me, wiping the tears away. "I just don't want you to get sucked back into those boys again. Sam is a great guy, and after you hear his messages you will agree, but I'm being selfish. Plus, I think Quick is better than any of them. I am a little biased. He might not have all that Sam has, but he would never hurt or harm you or Bella."

I grab her hands to reassure her. "I really like Quick. If we keep talking and it works out cool, but once I get on that plane my focus is going to be my divorce and my Bella Bug. And, to put your mind at ease, I will never be with Sam. No matter how sexy he may be."

We both laugh.

"Plus, I love this life you have made for yourself, and I'm kind of wanting my sister back too. If this job works out, I don't see why I can't move back. This weekend being around all you women, seeing how independent you all are has pulled me from my despair and I'm ready to fight for my happiness."

"I want to come back with you for a while," Izzy blurts out.

"I'll be fine. You need to keep DJing and what would Gus do without you?" I tease.

Izzy's face gets serious. "I'm just worried for you with Brody. The things he was saying on your voicemail. I told Gus I want someone to go back with you."

I laugh. "It's Brody. He talks a big talk."

"Rube, it's either me or one of the guys that goes back with you," Izzy states and before I can reply, she stops me. "Just for the first two days. I don't DJ until Thursday this week. I can come see Bella, your aunt, and make sure Brody is going to behave."

I know I can't change her mind, so I nod in agreement. Izzy squeals. "Good, I already booked my flight with yours."

We both laugh. And just like that, everything is okay. I do feel my chest get lighter knowing Izzy will be there just in case my newly found strength doesn't hold up to Brody's bullshit. Every time I think of Brody now, Quick replaces that thought with something good.

After spending the day with the girls again, all my mind has been doing is thinking about what ifs and us moving here. I went over all the stuff Eva gave me yesterday, and I even listened to some of the demos while Izzy was in the shower. That way when I speak with Luc tonight, I'll know what the hell I'm talking about and maybe even have some feedback on a few of these demos.

An hour later, Izzy and I are ready, and we're taking a shot in the kitchen when the doorbell rings with Gus and Quick strolling through it. Gus is the first to walk into the kitchen wearing what looks like swat gear, but when Quick moves from behind him, my mouth drops open. Looking nothing like Gus, Quick is wearing a pair of dark grey slacks with a light grey button-down shirt. He looks more like a model off the GQ magazine than someone on the swat team.

"Fuck me," I say breathily.

I can't take my eyes off Quick who's stalking toward me with the same carnal look on his face that I'm sure is plastered across mine. My body explodes with desire which gives me all the feelings of a cat in heat. I want to claw, nip, and bite him before I mount that fine ass of his.

With a sexy little smirk, he laughs. "Easy, Firecracker." As he engulfs me into a hug, my pussy spasms just from the smell of him. I take another deep breath inhaling more of him. Quick whispers into my ear, "If I fuck you now, we won't be leaving anytime soon."

I don't fucking care at this point. My body is primed and ready, he has my core humming for him. He releases me taking a step back so he can look me over as he licks his lips. "Goddamn, woman you're going to have my dick hard all night wearing that dress."

My heart swells with joy, feeling sexy as ever in Izzy's dress. It's a navy blue bodycon dress, the ones that are like a second skin they're so tight. Izzy did my makeup, while I did my hair, which is bone straight.

"Why're you so dressed up tonight?" I look between Gus and Quick wondering why they both look completely opposite.

"Redman has to work tonight as security. The club has a dress code so no cuts," Quick answers, still looking down at me like he wants to eat me.

"Where is everyone else?" Izzy questions from behind Quick.

"They're meeting us there. Mac needed Shy to stop by the White Wolf before coming," Gus answers, taking a water from the fridge.

"Okay, then are we ready? We still need to load up my DJ stuff," Izzy says, making her way to the living room.

Quick and I still in a trance, don't move. His recently showered hair falls into his face covering one eye, and without a thought, I reach my hand up scooting it back as I palm his face. Neither one of us say a word but instead just stare into each other's eyes, his are filled with so much emotion it has my inner thighs dampening.

"Let's go lovebirds," Izzy yells from the front door.

Quick leans down kissing me briefly before grabbing my hand to tug me along with him.

Tonight is going to be epic.

CHAPTER SIXTEEN

When we arrived at Club Spin, my heart felt like it was going to explode with so much excitement. Seeing all the people in line to get in, everyone was screaming Izzy's name. I couldn't stop smiling. I was so happy for her and how far she's come as a DJ. Entering the club, the vibration from the base echoing off the walls had me instantly moving my body to the beat. Izzy said the guy DJing was named DJ Rex and that he was the guy Eva had a thing for.

Being in a band having people crowd you was normal for me but the club life compared to band life were two different things. My body felt so alive and energized, like I was shocked back to life. Quick led me through the crowd, not letting anyone get too close. The security team that surrounded us was unmovable as they made a pathway for us to the VIP area.

When we reached the VIP area, it too was crowded, but I guess it was people from the label company. Izzy hugged a bunch of people, stopping to introduce me, and when I finally saw Luc and Mia approaching us, I became nervous. I know I've met them before, but that was before I knew they wanted to interview me. But as soon as Mia was close enough, she grabbed me for a hug, saying hello. Mia is the same height as me, so it's easy to hear her greet me. I hug her back by giving her an extra squeeze.

Luc follows suit as he leans down, hugging both Izzy and me before reaching his hand out to Quick who I seem to have forgotten was behind me. He rests his hand at my lower back giving me the support I need letting me know he is there.

Luc guides us over to his table, pouring us all a drink and cheers to a great night. My heart overflows with happiness. These people are so nice and inviting it has me wanting to cry. Luc and Quick start to discuss White Wolf lounge as Izzy pulls me to the side with Mia following us. "When I go on stage later I want you to stay here with Mia and the girls, who will be here soon."

Mia steps to my side. "Yes, sweetie, stay here with me, and we can talk with Lucas about the job we think would be a good fit for you."

My smile is from ear to ear as I say, "Okay, sounds good."

Mia and Izzy start talking about Alexandria and how her tour's going and when she will be back, but I just take in my surroundings. Watching all the people in the VIP area, the dance floor and all the booths that line the club. When I look to the stage, I see a medium built guy volleying from foot to foot as he plays with the mixer in front of him. I notice Eva move next to him and I smile. They look cute together.

"What has you smiling so big?" Quick asks, kissing my neck as he grips my hips from behind.

I point to the stage. "Eva and her guy. They look cute together."

As I turn into Quick's embrace, he looks at the stage and then back down to me. "We look good together don't you think?"

I giggle. "Yes, we do. I can't figure out if I like your bad boy biker look or this GQ model look you got going on right now."

Quick throws his head back with a deep laugh. *Jesus, he's beautiful.*

"Well, my little Firecracker, I hate to tell you this, but this bad boy biker is still under this GQ look. You'll never take the biker out of me."

Placing my hands on his chest, I smile up at him deviously. "Thank God. I think I'm fonder of the bad boy myself," I say teasingly.

As the night went on, the crowd grew in size with Ginger and Shy arriving along with a bunch of club members, which included Maze. She had the night off and was looking sexy as sin in her tiny silver dress. The men looked different without their cuts. When I asked where Mac was, they informed me he was staying at White Wolf to deal with some issues they were having.

Izzy is on stage DJing right now, and I'm sitting with Quick on one side of Shy and me on the other. Ginger has been moving around the VIP chatting with people. I was following her chatting with everyone but needed a break. So many people and names I won't remember tomorrow.

The guys sat at the edge of the VIP where we can see the stage clearly, as we watch Izzy bounce around. She really is so beautiful. Gus is stationed behind her looking scary as fuck and watching the crowd. I'm leaning back in my chair finishing my drink when Ginger dances over, standing in front of Shy swaying her hips.

"Hi, babe. Whatcha doing?" Ginger seductively leans down as she bends at the waist grabbing his thighs.

Shy who hasn't taken his eyes off his girl since they got here, smiles up at her. "Watching your fine ass move around in those tight leather pants, making my dick hard. Thinking I might need to take you in the bathroom for a quickie before you head on stage," he says matter of fact.

Quick who has been moving in his seat to the music, he grabs the bottle and pours me another drink. When he hands me my drink, Ginger straighten's up with a squeal. I sit forward waiting for something to happen and then Quick jumps up too. I'm about ready to jump up, but they look at each other and scream, "What the fuck?"

I move back relaxing into the couch next to Shy who hasn't moved but is laughing at them being fools. The song, "Loca People" by Sak Noel sounds through the club, and the crowd mimics them screaming the same thing.

Shy leans in toward me. "They do this all the time. My brother here is a dancing machine. He usually is all over the place." I love how energetic he is and doesn't care what anyone thinks. I start to feel bad.

"Has he been sitting here all night because of me? He can go dance if he wants. I feel bad now."

Shy turns to face me. "Firecracker, you need to chill out. That's not what I was saying." He chuckles. "I'm just saying they freak out all the time with music, just sit back and watch like I do." Shy pauses. "Unless you want to jump up and dance with them." He leans back laughing.

I smile at him but don't say anything. Instead, I sit back taking a sip of my drink.

Shy begins to talk, watching Quick as he speaks. "Ruby, I've never seen my brother act this way toward any woman before. We're close and-"

I interrupt him before he continues. "I know, Shy. Everyone has told me how he doesn't do relationships. How he doesn't date anyone twice. I've told him this is just a weekend thing, but he keeps telling me-"

Shy sits up turning his body so no one can see his demeanor change but when I do I snap my mouth shut with a gasp.

"Goddamn, do you always spout off like that before a person is done talking? Jesus Christ, Quick picked a fucking great nickname for you. But I need you to shut the fuck up and listen."

I nod my head, too scared to open my mouth. Shy's body is tense as his jaw clenches. I have obviously pissed him off.

"What I was saying is, that we're close and I've never seen him this happy. I don't give a fuck what anyone else said to you. I know my brother, and you make him happy. Whatever you two have going on is between you and don't let anyone else get involved." Shy pauses looking over at the group of people dancing. When he looks back down to me his face has softened. "Ruby, you're special to two of our women and one of my best friends. The main one being my old lady. She's hell-bent on getting you to move here. I just wanted to tell you that you have my support. If you ever need us, just reach out to us. The MC will never let you down. I know you have to deal with a lot of shit when you get home, but at any time you need us, we are a phone call away."

Tears fill my eyes as his words hit me hard. The love he has for Ginger and Quick is overwhelming. I reach up wiping a tear away and smile. "Thank you, Shy. That means more to me than you'll ever know."

Taking a couple deep breaths, I compose myself before Shy moves to lean back into the couch giving me full view of our crazy group dancing. I'm envious of the bond these people have together. I start to let my mind wander with all my what ifs and I begin to freak out. I start to panic. "Shy, I'm scared. What if I'm not good enough for him? What if I can't move here? What if he gets hurt? What if-"

Shy stops me, putting his hand up. "Wow, Firecracker. Slow down before you have everyone running over here worried about you. Take a deep breath." Shy moves to refill our drinks turning toward me again he says with soft eyes. "Ruby, you have a lot of shit going on in that little head of yours, but you need to think, what you can fix right now? What do you have control over right now? Who the fuck knows what tomorrow will bring. You can't stress out about tomorrow. Quick's a grown man, and he knows what he wants. He knows your situation. If he wants to dive in with you, then let him. Don't push people away who want to be there for you. If you do, you'll always be alone."

I take a big gulp of my drink and choke when I realize he made me a stiff drink. He tilts his head back with a laugh. I join in after my choking spell ends. As I look at Shy, feeling better, I say, "I'm scared shitless. I'm always scared I'll make the wrong decision."

Shy leans forward onto his elbow. "Don't be scared to live life. Fucking up is the best part." Shy chuckles, slamming his drink back. "You live, you learn, and you move on to the next thing life throws at you. Being scared is okay because it's a challenge. Challenges are a way of life. The more you overcome, the better you become."

Seeing our group make their way back to us he finishes, "Ruby, like I said, we're always here for you. Let people help you because you need to trust in someone."

The lump in my throat keeps me from replying to him, so I give him a big smile and nod my thank you.

"Iz is killing it on the decks tonight," Ginger exclaims as she grabs her drink taking a big sip.

Quick plops down next to me giving me a kiss on the cheek as Maze grabs a water from the bucket.

I smile at everyone taking another drink, trying to hide

my facial expression. Ginger, not missing a beat asks, "So what were you two talking about? It looked pretty serious?"

Shy leans forward grabbing Ginger around the waist, pulling her in between his legs. "Just life and making fun of your crazy asses bouncing around."

I stand up excusing myself saying I need to use the bathroom. I needed a minute to collect my thoughts, letting everything that Shy said sink in and pull myself together. Ginger and Maze say they need to go too and lead the way.

Ginger takes us the bathroom next to the stage that is only used for DJs and performers. Once we're in the empty bathroom, Ginger turns on me. "Okay, what did Shy say to you that freaked you out. I swear if he was mean to you or-"

I put my hand up stopping her from talking.

"He was very sweet. I was the asshole who interrupted him." Maze's face had me pausing to laugh. "Yes, I found out that you don't interrupt him while he is speaking. I think that was the only time I was freaked out, but he was still nice to me. He let me know I can count on the club if I ever need them."

Ginger's face lights up. "Thank God. I was going to cut him off from getting any if he was mean. Now he just earned himself a blowjob." All of us start to laugh. Ginger gives me a big hug. "Ruby, I really want you to come back here and live. I know you have to deal with some major stuff back home but know we are here."

I give her a big hug back trying to hold back the tears. "Dammit. I can't cry. No crying tonight," I cry out, wiping the tears.

"Okay, are we good? Can we go dance and get fucked up? It's your last night, and I took the night off. Let's have some fun. No more talk of sad shit," Maze demands.

We all laugh and go about our business getting freshened

up. Opening the door, Quick is pacing in front of the door with Gus standing guard.

"Jesus Christ. I was just about ready to charge in there. You bitches take forever," Quick ranted, charging over to me.

Seeing Gus standing there looking worried, I panic. "What's wrong?" I see Gus and freak out something happened to Izzy. "Where is Izzy?"

Gus puts his hand up. "She was worried about ya, so I came to check on ya."

Relief washes over me. "Thank God. I'm fine. We were just gossiping. All is good." I turn to Maze, grabbing her hand. "Let's go dance." Pulling her and Ginger to the dance floor.

The dance floor is packed like sardines, so we make our way to the front of the VIP booth. Gus makes his way back up to Izzy reporting I'm fine and when she sees us girls dancing she waves. Quick is giving us some space staying idly by watching over us girls.

It feels good just to let go and dance. As I tilt my head up toward the ceiling, I close my eyes and just relax as I move to the beat, letting the music take over my mind, body, and soul. I have forgotten how therapeutic dancing can be, not just on a pole but dancing period. Helps clean the soul, filling it with good energy and happy vibes. Five songs later, I have a sheen of sweat glistening over my body, with all the heat from the bodies dancing together.

"Sexy Bitch" by David Guetta featuring Akon, mixes in as I feel hands slide around my waist. Opening my eyes, I see Eva, Ginger, and Maze dancing in front of me with the men circling around us dancing. I grab Quick's hand pulling him closer to my back as we move as one. The dance floor has become even more crowded. The men have circled us girls so no one can hit on us, but with the masses of people, it gets hard.

"Damn girl. The way your body moves," Quick breathes into my ear. I lift both of my arms up behind my head sliding them around his neck as he leans down kissing my collarbone. Quick growls, pressing his cock into my ass as we sway to the song. Forgetting everyone else around us, letting the music take us on a journey.

Turning me around, Quick slides his hands down over my ass securing my dress from riding up as I entwine my fingers in his hair at the nape of his neck. Quick leans down kissing me, sliding a thigh between my legs taking control of our movements. The friction between my legs has me moaning for more. The atmosphere in the club has me feeling high, the lights flashing along with the smoke machine and the mass of people dancing. I feel out of control as we lose ourselves in the music. I give all control to Quick closing my eyes, letting the music fill my soul.

A half-hour later our clothes are damp with sweat. "I could dance all night with you. Your body is perfect for me. Goddamn, Firecracker, I'm so fucking hard right now." He groans into my neck.

I lean up on my tiptoes licking his sweaty neck before biting his earlobe. "Take me."

Quick looks down making sure he heard me correctly.

I smile. "Now."

He grabs my hand and pulls me off the dance floor rushing us to the bathroom. Quick closes the door, locking it and moves us to the counter. "This is going to be quick. Izzy gets off in five minutes and will need to use the restroom."

"Hurry," I whine.

Lifting my dress, I slip my panties off, handing them to Quick. He has his pants open and a condom on in seconds. I turn my back to him looking at him through the mirror as he moves behind me, he bends down placing his cock at my entrance. Gripping my hips, he thrusts up bottoming out in one motion with my pussy slick with desire.

"Jesus. This pussy is like crack. My dick craves it." He grunts with his massive thrust.

"Quick. Oh, God," I grit through clenched teeth.

I hold onto the counter for support as he leans me forward, bending me over the counter giving himself a different angle. Pounding harder, he goes deeper. "Look at me. Watch me fuck you," he demands, working me faster.

As I open my eyes, I see him devouring my body with his eyes. Quick reaches in front of me pulling one of my breasts out wrenching it as I cry out in pleasure.

"Fuck me. Harder," I moan.

Quick, who's watching his cock glides into my pussy, as he bites his lower lip.

"Harder?" he asks, still fixated at our connection.

"Yes, fuck me harder."

Quick breaks his stare as he looks up, so he can grab a handful of my hair, yanking it back, making me arch my back as he hammers his cock into my tightening pussy. My orgasm's at the brink of explosion, as I moan with each thrust.

Quick pulls me away from the counter thrusting up as he yanks my hair back, using his other hand, he slides it down the front of me cupping my mound as he fingers my clit. I scream my release as my walls spasm around his thick cock.

Quick releases me, pushing me up against the counter as he lifts one of my legs, as he pins me down jacking his cock harder and deeper into my pussy. Keeping my eyes on him, I see his neck muscle tighten with each pump. He's close to his own climax. I reach back with one hand cupping his balls.

"Oh, yeah." Quick throws his head back groaning his release as he slows his thrust. He releases my leg letting me stand up. Quick still hasn't withdrawn from inside me. Gripping my hips, he leans down biting my shoulder. "Firecracker. I don't know what I'm going to do when you leave," he confesses.

Lost in my own sated state, I don't reply but just smile. Quick pumps a couple more times before he slips out, disposing of the condom, while I put myself back together and freshen up.

As Quick fixes himself, he stands behind me hugging me and placing soft kisses along my shoulder and neck.

A knock at the door has me giggling, as we move to leave the bathroom.

Izzy yells, "Bitch you better be getting some in there," from the other side of the door.

I open the door with a huge smile.

"Thatta girl. Get some." Izzy laughs.

I hug her as she moves into the bathroom.

"I got to pee. Bye, Quick," she exclaims.

Izzy yammers about her set and the crowd and I tune her out looking at myself in the mirror. My lips are swollen from kissing, and my cheeks are flushed from being fucked properly. I giggle feeling my lips with my fingertips. Izzy comes out of the bathroom and takes one look at me before busting up laughing.

"Damn girl. You got fucked good," Izzy laughs.

I reply by nodding my head, still feeling my swollen lips.

"Well, snap out of it, Luc is waiting to talk to you so pull yourself together. Here, I have some makeup let's freshen you up, hoe." Izzy is beaming.

Ten minutes later we're in the VIP area talking to Luc and Mia about my future with Spin It Inc. I'm so glad I listened to a few demos and went over the application. Luc is a great businessman and definitely knows his shit.

I can tell he did some research on me as well because he asked a bunch of questions about the band and their touring details.

In the back of my mind, I wonder if he's also seen the file the club has on me. He seems to know a lot about me. Izzy and Eva are here with me, but they let me do all the talking. The more I speak with Luc, the more comfortable I am with him and begin to really explain what I used to do for the band. Well, before Bella was born. We've kept it all business so far, and I'm beaming with joy from the sound of this job I'll really like it.

I watch the boys sitting to the side having a conversation while we chat with Luc. Quick never takes his eyes off of me, and when our eyes lock, I give him a brief smile.

"Ruby, I have to ask since I don't know all the details, but what're your plans? Izzy said divorce, yeah? Maybe relocate?" Luc inquires.

"I'm for sure getting a divorce. Depending on how difficult he will make it and finances, that will determine if I can move," I reply hesitantly.

Izzy wants to say something, but I give her a look telling her not to get involved. I know she wants to say she will pay for us to move here but it's more than that.

"I know it's none of our business, but once you become an employee, we take care of our people. We can help if you need it. I have no problem with you workin' from LA, but that would include a lot of travel for you. If you're as good as I think you are, I'll want you to travel with some performers. Will that be a problem?"

I shake my head. "No, I have support back home, and that is something I would need to figure out before I move here."

Eva says enthusiastically, "Well, I can help with all that. One, we have a daycare on site at the building."

Mia's next to pipe in with, "I'm sure I'll be able to help out too. I love kids."

"Again, I know you have a lot to think about and decisions that need to be made, but just know you will have all the support you need once you move here. Next Monday give Mia a call and let us know what you decide, and we can start there and see how that goes," Luc explains.

"Thank you. Thank you so much. I really want this job. It seems perfect for me. I just need to figure things out regarding Bella before I jump in," I reply.

Luc laughs, showing his beautiful smile. "I think you will be perfect for the job as well."

Izzy and Eva both squeal while Mia gives me a hug. I feel so empowered. My gut tells me this company is my future. I smile looking around at all the people in the VIP area. I can see myself here. When my eyes land on Quick again my heart skips. The look on his face is nothing but happiness. He is genuinely excited for me, and he has done nothing today but give me encouraging words.

As I make my way back over to him I tell myself, *I've got tonight. That's all I've got - one more night.*

CHAPTER SEVENTEEN

We've all returned to the clubhouse after Ginger finished her set at the club. The rest of the night was pure bliss, like something out of a movie. I'm so scared that tomorrow when I get on that plane this will all be just a dream. The life that I've always wanted at my fingertips.

I look over to see Ginger dancing in front of Shy seductively. There're about fifteen or so hanging out on the second floor listening to music. Mac and Dallas arrived with about five girls from the White Wolf. Two of the girls are on the stage dancing around giving the boys a show. Maze is sitting on a member name Tiny's lap while the rest of us are lounging on couches. The men are relaxed being back at the club. Izzy, Gus, Quick, and myself are on one big couch while Shy and Ginger are in a wide lounge chair.

I feel like I belong here and my heart hurts for tomorrow. I snuggle deeper into Quick, who has his arm around me. My heels are off and I'm curled up with my legs under me as I lean into Quick. Gus and Izzy seem to be arguing over her coming to LA with me. I told her she doesn't have to come, but she told Luc she was going but will be back before her show Thursday, giving her three days to help me. She told Gus on the way home that she was going, and he isn't too happy. The boys seem to think they should be able to come too. Gus's using the bodyguard card, but I think it's making it worse since she feels they are more. They really need to figure their shit out. It's confusing as all hell to everyone else around.

"Firecracker, you almost ready to head upstairs? I've shared you long enough. I need my time with you," Quick murmurs into my ear sending an electric charge straight to my core.

I nod my head with an, "Uh-huh."

Quick's swift movement has me up in his arms holding my heels as he announces we're headed to bed. I wrap my arms around his neck, saying my goodbyes to everyone. Our plan is to all have lunch together before we head to the airport.

Once we're in the elevator, Quick shifts me so I'm straddling him with my legs wrapped around his waist. He grips my ass pinning me against the elevator wall. "Goddamn, I've been wanting to be alone with you all fucking day. That quickie at the club only made me want you more," Quick says before kissing me. The elevator door dings, breaking our kiss.

Quick places me on my feet inside his door, locking it behind him. I'm about to take my dress off when Quick says huskily, "Don't move. Don't take anything off. Just stand there."

I freeze from taking my dress off but turn to face him as he takes his shirt off. The light in the room is dim giving it a romantic setting. My pussy pulses like a cry for help. I shift from one foot to another trying to help relieve some pressure, feeling wetness between my thighs. Quick never gave me my panties back from the bathroom, leaving me pantiless. He's been torturing me with a swipe of his fingers over my clit throughout the night while no one was watching. Keeping me aroused and wet all night. Now I'm just dripping with need.

Quick strips his clothes while watching me stand there getting aroused. I lick my lips biting down, feeling the pain as pleasurable.

"Close your eyes," he says in a commanding voice.

I do as he says taking a deep breath. I feel Quick's fingertips graze over my chest shifting my hair back over my shoulders exposing my neck. He leans in placing butterfly kisses along my collarbone and up my neck. I moan feeling my body shiver.

Quick grabs the hem of my dress, lifting it up over my head. "I want to cherish every inch of you tonight. I want to memorize every crevice of your beautiful body." He breathes against my skin as his fingers caress along my body.

"Yes," I say in a whisper.

Unclasping my bra, Quick slowly slips each strap off my shoulders one shoulder at a time. "I want you to know how much I want you and how special you are to me," he says inches away from my ear sending a heat wave over my body.

Gripping my hips, Quick guides me to the bed positioning me on my back before placing himself between my legs. Starting with my neck, Quick licks, sucks, and kisses, moving slowly down my body. Capturing each nipple torturing each one, I moan my approval, lifting my back off the bed. Quick glides his fingers up and down my stomach and back to my core.

"Please. Fuck me," I whine desperately.

He releases my breast with a pop. "I've been dying to do something with you. It goes against my number one rule, but you're special. I need to know before you leave."

Right now, I would agree to anything he asked of me just as long as he let me climax. "Hmmm? What?"

Quick stops touching me as he moves to lay next to me, I open my eyes, desperate for his touch. Quick stares down at me as he cups my cheek. "I want to take you bare. I want to mark you in every way I can before you leave. I want to feel your skin against my skin. Your pussy's so hot that I want to feel it smolder around my cock."

I turn my body, so we're facing each other. I lay there for a second looking into his eyes, seeing the desire and passion he has for me. I nod my head. "Okay."

Quick's face breaks out into a huge smile. "Are you protected?" Quick asks eagerly.

I nod my head again. "I haven't been with anyone since Brody which was right after the incident. I was checked twice since then. I've only been with Brody and well Sam, but he wore a condom and now you," I explain.

Quick groans. "Jesus Christ. I want you so fucking bad."

Quick grabs my waist pulling me closer, kissing me deep with long strokes. I get a burst of courage and push Quick to his back, straddling him. My hair falls forward covering both of us, so I break the kiss, raising up, reaching between us and positioning his cock at my entrance.

"Ride me, Firecracker." He grins, biting his lip as he slides his hands up my thighs, waiting for me to descend. Feeling the warmth of his cock has my pussy spasming. I slowly work my way down only to pump up a bit, lubing his cock as I seat myself upon him. "Fuck. Ruby," Quick grits out watching me smother his dick. We're both panting.

"Fuck you need to move, or I'm going to come real fast. Goddamn, your pussy feels fucking good wrapped around my cock." Quick grabs my hips moving me forward and back, so I lift up and slam down hard against him.

We both cry out, "Fuck yeah."

My God he feels so fucking good.

That is all it took for me, and I start to ride him. I shift my hips forward and back thrusting hard, taking him deep, hitting my cervix.

"That's it my little gem. Ride my cock, Rube. Fuck me, baby." He drops his head back as he digs his nails deep into my hips.

Moaning with each thrust, I grab the headboard behind him riding him harder and faster.

Quick is grunting "yeah" over and over. His cock thickens within me, feeling it pulse as he reaches his climax. His neck muscles bulge out, and his face turns red. "Jesus Christ." He starts to thrust his cock up meeting my thrust.

"Fuck yeah. Yeah. ah…" I scream out, collapsing forward holding onto the headboard, as my legs start to cramp up from the orgasm rippling through me.

Quick's like lightning flipping us over as he stays seated in me. He doesn't miss a beat as he continues to pump into me with fast, sharp thrusts as sweat drips from his face.

"Fuck Ruby. I'm close." Quick's face is beet red with sweat-drenched hair sticking to his forehead.

"Quick, harder," I whine.

"Your pussy. Jesus, it feels. So fucking good, baby. Fuu-uck."

My climax shoots through me, hearing his words I lose control orgasming again around his thickness clenching each inch of his shaft, coating it with each thrust. I hear sloshing sounds of my come sliding down to my asshole.

"Goddamn, your cock is so fucking big," I say.

"Fuck yeah. Keep talking." He rams me harder with a couple sharp pumps before he loses control jacking his cock into me so fast that my tits are flying everywhere.

I feel so wild and alive. It's like he's my freedom. I'm fucking free. "Fuck me hard. Claim my pussy," I demand. Quick leans back grabbing my legs as he lifts my ass off the bed hammering me deeper, engulfing his cock so it hits my cervix.

"Oh, fuck..." I moan, arching my back off the bed, leaving only my head touching the bed as another orgasm soars through me. My walls contract around his dick sending him over the edge as his climax hits him hard.

Quick's head drops back, his hands become a vise, gripping my body as he shudders above me moaning his release. I feel his warm come squirt deep inside filling me, making my body quiver as he pumps long, deep, thrusts.

"Jesus Christ. Milk my cock, Ruby." Quick drops down over me taking my mouth hard, devouring me, he breaks for a breath, panting with each thrust. He puts all his weight on me sucking my neck as he continues moving in and out, slowly with each thrust. When he stops, still fully inside me, he breaks the suck releasing my neck. Like he's a vampire sucking every last ounce of blood from me, I feel dizzy. Neither one of us speak but just lay there letting the waves of emotion crash through us, leaving us both in a slumbering state.

CHAPTER EIGHTEEN

"What's wrong with you? Are you hungover?" Izzy asks when she approaches me sitting at the bar downstairs.

I peer at her from over my coffee mug. "I'm tired as fuck, and I can't move," I grumble.

Maze laughs from across the bar. "She barely made it to the bar stool. Quick had to help her."

"Seriously? What did he do to you?" Izzy laughs.

I place my head on the bar. "Let's just say he made sure to touch *every* inch of my body and leave *plenty* of marks on me."

"Shut the fuck up? Let me see," Izzy demands, standing up moving next to me, pulling my head off the bar evaluating me. "Oh. My. God." She's shocked when she sees all the hickeys across my chest and neck.

"Where is Quick?" she asks, looking around trying to hide her amusement.

I point over my shoulder to the end of the hall. "Meeting with Shy."

"Are you mad?" Izzy is trying to be concerned but is failing horribly.

I smile for the first time. "No, it was the best night of my life, but if I don't have sex for a month, I think I'll be okay."

"Well, I'm sure that's what he was going for." She laughs, sitting back down. "But damn those hickeys could of been a bit lower. There is no hiding those bad boys."

Quick did what he promised last night and explored every inch of my body. Fucking and sucking every entrance my body allowed. He devoured me like a crazed man obsessed, with all the positions he put me in last night and again this morning in the shower.

My pussy was so raw and swollen that he could only take me from behind this morning in the shower. Before we got dressed, he sucked my pussy one last time to say his goodbye.

I've never, even on drugs, had that many orgasms. He was like a cat in heat with his cock never going soft longer than a few minutes before he wanted more. He was insatiable, only sleeping in small increments before pouncing on me again. He even fell asleep inside me a couple times. It was the best night of my life.

"He went a little crazy in the shower this morning with sucking," I explain with a smile remembering.

Both girls say in unison with a laugh, "I bet he did."

As the men start to emerge from the clubroom Ginger and Izzy watched as Quick strode toward us.

"He doesn't look hurt like you do, Rube," Izzy states loud enough for everyone to hear.

"Wait 'til you see his neck," Dallas bellows from behind Quick.

Quick flips everyone off laughing. As I turn around on my stool, I smile, feeling all warm inside as he stalks toward me.

"Jesus Christ! Quick, we might need to fucking rename

you to Hoover. Fuck, did you mark her enough? Everyone will know she was fucked good last night," Mac says standing next to me looking at all the hickeys on my neck.

"I wanted to make sure she wouldn't forget me. Fucked her so hard she won't need any sex for a few weeks before I can come see her." Quick leans down kissing me. "Right, Firecracker?"

But before I can say anything, Izzy leans in close to us. "You're planning on going to visit her soon?"

We both look over to Izzy and nod our heads.

"Fuck yeah. I won't be able to stay away more than a week - two at the most. Before I will need my fix," Quick states with a chuckle.

I hope he does, but I'm not holding my breath. I'm still in a happy bubble from last night, and anything sounds good right now, but tomorrow is a different day.

We'll see if he still remembers me.

Izzy stands up. "Okay, let's go try to cover up some of these marks before we go into public."

Everyone laughs as they see me try to stand up and move to the bathroom. My body isn't working. It hurts everywhere.

About twenty of us headed to a restaurant for some lunch before the four of us had to head to the airport. Lunch was filled with a lot of laughter, heckles, and jokes. I felt my heart was overflowing with so much happiness spilling over, that I tried to soak up as much as I could before I had to head back to my life.

I cried as everyone hugged me telling me they couldn't wait to see me again. That I needed to move here, and I cried from all the love and support they showed me. I was going to miss them.

Gus drove us with Quick and I sitting in the back of the

SUV. The exhaustion from no sleep the night before starts to kick in as I yawn.

"I'll text you later. I know Izzy isn't giving you your phone 'til you get on the plane, but I already got your cell number. If you need any help just call, like Shy said, we're here for you," Quick rambles next to me.

I smile up at him nodding my head. When I don't speak, he turns in his seat to face me.

"What are you thinking?" he pleads with me.

"Just I have a lot of shit to deal with, and I don't want you to feel you have to keep in contact with me. This was a great weekend, and I loved every minute of it, but I don't expect you to wait for me," I say honestly.

Quick's face turns hard. "Do you not want me to keep in touch?"

I sigh. "No, that isn't what I'm saying. I do want you to keep in touch. I just don't want you to feel bad if some girl comes along at the club and you want to fuck her."

"My dick's so raw that I don't think I would be able to fuck even if I wanted to. I seriously need to give my buddy a rest. Plus, I think you ruined me for other women, but I hear what you're saying." Quick laughs. He grabs my hands. "I feel like a fucking pussy right now. I don't want you to leave, but I know you have to. I'm just so glad I decided to take Redman to the airport, and we met. I hope that, if anything, we'll stay in touch and see what happens. That's all I want." Quick leans in, kissing me.

My heart hurts. These past four days with the Wolfeman MC, Izzy, and Quick have been the best of my life. My life I dreamt of having and pray I will be able to make a reality. I just need to stay focused.

"Quick, I'm so glad we met, and I hope we can make it

work too. Just be patient with me, and we'll see where we go," I murmur, deepening the kiss.

Fuck, I'm going to miss his kisses.

When we approach the airport, everyone gets out, and the boys pull our bags out from the back. I move to give Gus a big hug and kiss on the cheek saying goodbye. Quick moves to the curb picking me up, giving me one of his breathtaking kisses.

"Don't forget me, Firecracker," he whispers against my lips.

I answer with a kiss, "Never going to happen."

He kisses me one last time before releasing me.

"I'll text you once I get my phone back." I smile.

Gus has Izzy in a bear hug kissing her neck saying something into her ear. When he releases her, she cups his cheek with her hand before turning to leave. The look on her face has me worried, but I don't say anything. Instead, I turn to head inside, leaving the man of my dreams behind to deal with the pain of my existence.

This has been the best weekend of my life. I'm looking forward to the next chapter that is in store for my future.

The End... for now.

Ruby and Quick's full-length story will continue in the first book in The Wolfeman MC series. Coming soon.

ABOUT THE AUTHOR

Crazy, outgoing, adventurous, full of energy and talks faster than an auctioneer with a heart as big as the ocean... that is Angera. A born and raised California native, Angera is currently living and working in the Bay Area. Mom of a smart and sassy little girl, an English bulldog, and two Siamese Cats. She spends her days running a successful law firm but in her spare time enjoys writing, reading, dancing, playing softball, spending time with family and making friends wherever she goes. She started writing after the birth of her daughter in 2012 and hasn't been able to turn the voices off yet. The Spin It series is inspired by the several years Angera spent married into the world of underground music and her undeniable love of dirty and gritty romance novels.

ALSO BY ANGERA ALLEN

SPIN IT SERIES

Alexandria – Book One

Ginger – Book Two

COMING SOON

Izzy – Book Three – Spin It Series
Quick – Book One – The Wolfeman MC Series

FOLLOW AND CONNECT

Email ~ authorangeraallen@gmail.com
Website ~ authorangeraallen.com
Facebook ~ /authorangeraallen
Instagram ~ @angeraallen
Twitter ~ @angeraallen

Available ~ Amazon – iBooks – Nook – Kobo

ACKNOWLEDGMENTS

This last year has been a crazy ride. Ruby's story started out to be a 15k for a anthology for Shameless Book Con, but once Ruby's story started, I couldn't stop. To finish her book, I would have had to spoil most of Izzy's story, so I had to cut it off with just a crazy weekend. Her story will continue in the first installment of The Wolfeman MC series in Quick's story. I hate cliffhangers, but it was the only way. I promise Izzy and Quick's stories will be out before end of year.

Okay, as always, I want to first and foremost, thank my family most importantly my parents. They are my biggest fans and supporters. My father for all his love and support, especially his hugs. My mom has and will always be my biggest cheerleader and my best friend. My auntie Debbie for always being there for me. You always put a smile on my face no matter what is going on. I can't wait for our next girl's trip.

To my baby girl: Thank you for understanding Momma has to work on her computer at night. Your daily smiles, hugs and I love you's are priceless. The love and support you give to me is the strength I need to keep going. I love you, my little sunshine.

To my die-hard beta readers: Marlena S., Jennifer G., Kim H., Jennifer R., and Angie D. All of you ladies have been with me each step of the way, giving me honest advice and unwavering support. Thank you for always dropping what you are doing to read the newest chapters, and respond with your honest advice. I love each and every one of you.

Marlena Salinas, As always, you are my partner in crime and soul sister. I could be here all day listing all the things you have done for me throughout the years. You are my spiritual ground, and you always help me lighten my soul when it is full. I am so thankful for your true friendship. I love you Mar.

Kim Holtz, you always know what I am thinking, so thank you for fixing my mixed up words! I love that you can understand me even when I don't make sense. I look forward to all our upcoming book endeavors. You are one of my go-to girls whenever I need honest feedback. Thank you! Love ya, girl!

Jennifer Guibor, you are my savior. Thank you for always dropping whatever you are doing to read a new chapter. For all your honest opinion and your push to get the next chapters. Thank you, and I love ya, girl.

Angie Davis: Thank you for keeping my Angels group going strong with all the planning, building, scheduling of takeovers and daily devotion to the group. I love you girl, you've been my rock, and I couldn't do it without you. Thank you for all you do.

Heather Coker & Jennifer Ramsey: Thank you, ladies, for designing and making my swag. I love them! Both of you have been by my side through all of my books, and I am so grateful to have each of you in my life.

To all my guy friends who helped in making this book by giving me advice, doing "research" or stating the facts: N. Northrop, Worm, Baby J, and the MC next door I love you guys.

CT Cover Creations- Clarise Tan, thank you for being patient with me. You are brilliant, and I look forward to many more cover designs from you.

.

To my editor, Ellie McLove: Thank you for reading my words and making my story shine. I thank God you are amazing at what you do, and I look forward to many years of working together.

My bloggers: Book Happiness, Romance Book Worm, Jam Book Blog for pushing my cover and book release.

Give Me Books Promotions: Thank you for doing all the promotional giveaways, release blitz and boosts. I look forward to working with you more.

To my Angels, thank you for all your support and helping me build my dream. I love my group, and it just keeps getting bigger... let's keep it going!

Thank you to all my author friends who have helped me through this process with so much love, lots of patience and much needed support: S.R. Watson, Leela Lou Dahl, Chelle Bliss, Felicia Fox, Chelsea Camaron, Kathy Coopmans, Harper Sloan, Felicia Lynn, AD Justice, and Vicki Green.

To all my friends and family that have pushed me and supported me through this last year and a half, I just want you all to know I love you and thank God every day for you. Without your love and support, I wouldn't have been able to finish this book. I know I'm forgetting people, and I am sorry for that, but just know I am so thankful for everyone that had a part in making this dream a reality.

Last but definitely not least, to my fans. It has been

CRAZY with all the emails and reviews from my first couple books. I can't wait to see what you all think of Ruby. I love each and every one of you.

With Love, Angera

Made in the USA
Monee, IL
11 May 2022